X

Fraidy Ca

Fraidy Cats

S. S. Wilson

Based on a story by
Brent Maddock & S. S. Wilson

Real Deal Productions, Inc.

Copyright © 2013 S. S. Wilson

The moral right of the author has been asserted.

All rights reserved.
No part of this publication may be reproduced, stored in a retrieval system, or transmitted, in any form or by any means, without the prior permission in writing of the publisher, nor be otherwise circulated in any form of binding or cover other than that in which it is published and without a similar condition including this condition being imposed on the subsequent purchaser.

Published by Real Deal Productions, Inc.
P.O. Box 142
Wadsworth, IL 60083

Library of Congress Control Number 2013917471

ISBN 978-0-9827222-9-9

WIL
1743 8477   7/18/14   LCL
Wilson, S. S.

raidy cats
ABJ

CONTENTS

LeRoy Collins Leon County
Public Library System
200 West Park Avenue
Tallahassee, FL 32301

CHAPTER ONE

"I desperately want to leave this town," announced the rather high-strung Rolf. He was referring to the village of Dunkelhaven, nestled on the south bank of the Weser River in northern Germany. It was early spring. Winter had been hard, as it always was, and that added a layer of darkness to Rolf's mood.

Had he not made his remark, this story would have been quite different. Actually, it probably wouldn't have happened at all. But he did make it, so we are obligated to push on.

"Why?" asked his rather less-high-strung partner, Hermann.

This was a logical question, for it was 1810, way before 2010 and even way before 1910. At that time in Germany, one town was pretty much like another, and they didn't even call the area Germany yet, but that's beside the point. The point is, no town had electricity, running water, toilets, telephones, TVs, movie theaters or outlet malls. So there really wasn't much reason to go from one to another. Nevertheless, Rolf defended his opinion.

"Because I do not feel we are welcome here."

"But, my dear Rolf," queried Hermann, "do you suggest that we have ever been welcome *anywhere*?"

The question annoyed Rolf. He did not like being challenged on his announcements. But he and Hermann tried never to be sharp or angry with one another; they were the best of friends. So he answered civilly.

"It's simply that I have a new sense of added un-welcome-ness."

"Does your sense preclude our current search for food?" asked Hermann, a bit worried. He was always a bit worried that Rolf's sudden ideas and/or fits of temper would interrupt their more-or-less constant quest for something to eat.

"It does not, but it is something I wish to discuss further once we are well fed. Let us be off."

And so, to Hermann's relief, off they trotted down the alley, eyes alert, ears forward, tails straight up in the air.

We should mention here that Rolf and Hermann were cats, alley cats, if we must be accurate.

Rolf was lean and wiry. His short, compact fur was storm-cloud gray and lay close to his body, defined by his strong, ever-tense muscles. He had taller-than-average ears and longer-than average-whiskers. One whisker, on the left, was longer even than the others, giving him a sort of lopsided look when one faced him head on. This bothered him, of course, since he abhorred asymmetry, but a cat can't just go to a barber and get a whisker trim, so he was stuck with it. Strangely, he took little note of his most striking feature: he had narrow, almond-shaped blue eyes. This made him look either full of wisdom or full of wickedness, depending on one's reaction to eye shape. Hermann felt certain there was some Siamese in Rolf's ancestry, but he had the good taste not to bring it up.

To continue with our vaguely Asian references, Hermann was Yin to Rolf's Yang. Where Rolf was lean, Hermann was plump (he liked to say "solidly built"). Where Rolf's fur was short and gray, Hermann's was long, luxurious, and a painterly palette of glowing oranges and creams. He had small ears, almost lost in fur, a round face, and big, inviting eyes that were a stunning emerald green. On seeing him, one was forced to wonder why he had not been adopted by some loving family. This was because Rolf would not hear of it, and Hermann almost always abided by what Rolf dictated.

Incidentally, they were offended by the term "alley cats," for they saw themselves as quite sophisticated, worthy of being kings, or at least of being the cats of a king. That is why they addressed each other in so formal a manner.

In truth, their lives up to now had been rather less than kingly, or even princely, knightly or bishopy. Born to the alleys of Dunkelhaven, there they had remained.

At the end of this particular alley, they came upon a band of pigs who were eating fly-covered garbage in the street. This was a common sight. You see, way back then, people just threw all their trash and even their unmentionable stuff, which we'll not mention, into the streets in front of their houses. Roving pigs cleaned up some of it. Poor people picked through it for anything of value. But the rest just sat there. People hadn't gotten around to inventing trash collection because they were too busy starving, having wars, or getting small pox and the plague.

So this pig moment was part of every day life. Rolf and Hermann paid it no mind as they swerved wide around the snuffling creatures and continued up the street. Today was sunny, and Tuesday, and that meant that their quest took them to the neighborhood on the hill overlooking the river, the neighborhood of Dunkelhaven's well-to-do.

It was quite unlike the dank alleys and cramped, twisting streets of their usual haunts. Towering beeches and oaks shaded wide cobblestone avenues. There were few mud puddles and no unkempt bramble bushes. A cat could glide along for blocks under well-trimmed hedges and never pick up a single burr. Also, there were no pigs, for the well-to-do paid the less-well-off to carry garbage some place else, without caring particularly where that place was.

Every house was a multi-storied statement of wealth. Some were built of flame-red brick with meticulously painted decorative white trim. Others rose up in fine-cut blocks of the local yellowish stone. Still others wore an icing of rich white plaster whose glare hurt your eyes on a sunny day. All had slate roofs, steeply sloped to shed winter's snow.

As Rolf and Hermann padded comfortably from hedge to rose bush to topiary elephant, a cornucopia of delightful smells flitted around them like olfactory butterflies. There were aromas of flowers, fruit, fresh cut grass, hardwood smoke from kitchen fires, and food. Their favorite was food.

But they did not waste time chasing down random scents. No, they knew right where they were headed. The humans in one particular two-story red brick house always took a walk to the local park on Tuesdays, if the weather was nice. And, since the weather was nice, they always left certain windows open.

Furthermore, the young girl human of the house had as her pet a Bichon Frise (a small, white cotton-fluffy dog). Her parents kept on hand for this annoying canine an absolutely obscene amount of treats. So, on sunny summer Tuesdays it was always worth the hike up the hill to see if any of the treats could be lured out of the house.

The cats' timing was excellent. Just as they arrived, they saw the family walking away toward the park. The second floor windows were open. Perfect. They could put one of their standard plans into action.

Hermann always served as decoy. He leapt onto the front porch railing and began parading up and down in front of the living room windows. Invariably, the Bichon Frise was snoozing on the living room sofa and, invariably, it spotted him within seconds. The dog flew to the window, springing madly up and down, for he was too short to see out otherwise, and shouting hysterically, "Iseeyoustupidcat!! Iseeyou! Iseeyou! Iseeyou!" Small dogs shouted everything very fast. Hermann calmly continued parading and the dog reliably continued bouncing and shouting.

Rolf was thus free to glide unnoticed to the side of the house where grew a tall, finely-formed beech tree. Its branches nearly touched one of the aforementioned windows. Rolf flowed up the trunk, then along a branch, and made a graceful leap into the house.

He landed lightly on an ornate walnut desk in an equally ornate walnut paneled study. He glanced about and listened closely. The Bichon was still shrieking mindlessly at Hermann downstairs.

He hopped silently to the floor and peered out into the upstairs hall. The coast was still clear. So he slithered along the wall, past the doorways to two bedrooms, and then down the stairs. There he paused at the rear of the living room. The Bichon Frise, intent on his maniacal shouting at Hermann, did not notice him. The great thing about dogs was that, once excited about something, they made so much noise they couldn't hear anything else. Not a mistake a cat would make.

Rolf wasn't really afraid of the little dog, of course, He knew that, even if the Bichon spotted him, a loud spit and a show of tooth and claw would probably send the critter scampering under the sofa, but you always avoided a fight if you could. Fights waste time and sometimes cost fur. Rolf and Hermann prided themselves on the efficiency of their missions.

He moved across the living room and into the kitchen, where he began scanning for accessible containers. Immediately his nose told him something very good was nearby — smoked fish! A bit more searching pointed him to a high shelf. On it was a small wicker basket, placed that high, no doubt, to keep it out of the Bichon's reach. He took a moment to analyze the available surfaces — water barrel, counter top, wood stove, plate shelf, cupboard. Using them in that order, an easy series of leaps landed him on the shelf beside the basket.

He sniffed it. Fabulous! He took the handle in his teeth and lifted. The basket was awkward but not too heavy. He leapt down with it and headed back toward the living room. He tried to be quiet, but there was no way to keep the basket from dragging on the floor. The Bichon heard it even over his own frenzied barking. He whirled, wide-eyed, quivering as though made of springs. The pitch of his barking rose a full ear-splitting octave, "Iseeyoutoo! Iseeyoutooevilcat! Evilcat! Evilcat!"

Rolf grimaced. Now it would be a close race. He lurched up the stairs, basket clattering and bouncing. The dog shot across the living room in pursuit.

Rolf waddled as fast as possible past the upstairs bedrooms, rounding the turn into the study just inches ahead of the dog. But the dog, like all dogs, couldn't make the turn nearly as gracefully and went skidding helplessly down the hall on the waxed wooden floor. Rolf then had plenty of time to jump up onto the desk near the open window.

There he discovered a problem: the window wasn't open wide enough to fit the basket through.

By now the Bichon was hopping up and down beside the desk, shrieking, "Iseeyou! Ihateyou! Iseeyou! Ihateyou!" But he was too short to jump onto the desk, so Rolf ignored him in that really cool way cats do, and continued to study the problem.

After a moment's thought, he put his paws on the edge of the basket and carefully tipped it onto its side. The hinged top swung open and the contents spilled out onto the table — lots of delicious morsels of dried, smoked fish; haddock, to be exact.

Rolf now called out the window, "I say, Hermann!"

Hermann was already waiting at the base of the beech tree, having seen the Bichon go stampeding up the stairs, "Yes, Rolf?"

"I'm going to have to throw the food out a bit at a time. Can you catch it please?"

"Indeed I can," Hermann called back confidently. "And what is the food, pray tell?"

"It's that fish the humans dry out and sort of slightly burn."

"I *love* that fish!" exclaimed Hermann happily.

"Evilcats! Evilcats! Don'ttakeit! Don'ttakeit!" whined the unhappy Bichon.

Rolf spun about, arched his back and hissed loudly down at the little dog, "Can't you *ever* be quiet?!"

The Bichon shrank fearfully away from the desk and was silent for a moment. Then in a small voice he tried to make sound like a snarl, he said more slowly, "But the humans will blame *me*. They always blame me when you take things and make messes."

"You're the one who chooses to live with them" snapped Rolf. He aimed his butt at the open window, looked over his shoulder and began kicking out pieces of smoked fish with his hind legs. He was quite accurate.

Down below, Hermann leapt up and caught the first one right in his mouth. "Mmmmmmm!" The next one he caught and dutifully set aside for Rolf. And so it went, piece after piece. Gulp, one for him. Catch, one for Rolf. This was turning out to be one of their more successful raids.

Upstairs, as Rolf arranged more pieces in a row for his next volley, he and the Bichon suddenly heard breaking glass somewhere downstairs. The Bichon, a trembling snowball, whirled to face the open door of the study, "Whatwasthat? Whatwasthat?"

Now they heard heavy footsteps thudding rapidly up the stairs; then crashing and banging from the bedrooms down the hall.

"Whatisit?! *Who*isit?" whimpered the Bichon, edging toward the door, tail tucked. "It is not my masters, I know their step!"

Rolf didn't care who it was. He knew that he could make an instant escape out the window any time he wanted. So he determinedly kept kicking out smoked fish. Down below, Hermann merrily kept gulping and catching.

A moment later, two men burst into the study. They were dressed quite shabbily and obviously did not belong in this house of the well-to-do. Each man was carrying a cloth sack full of things that tinkled and jangled.

The first man tripped over the frozen Bichon, who was thereby booted right across the room, flying end-over-end, yike-yiking like some sort of furry firework. The tripped man toppled forward, arms splaying out, and crashed down on the desk.

As per back-up plan, Rolf was already gone. He'd launched himself straight as an arrow out the window and was half way down the beech tree.

As the man hit the desk, his sack flew open. Many things, in turn, flew out of it. Silver candlesticks, silver dinnerware, a clock, and jewelry. In that last category was a ring featuring a very large diamond. The man was horrified to see the ring sail right out the window.

Down below, Hermann sat happily, mouth open, waiting for the next piece of fish (since it happened to be his turn). The diamond ring landed right in his mouth. GULP. He swallowed it. Then he made a sour face, "Rolf, what are you doing up there?" he called. "That last piece tasted terrible!"

"I'm right beside you, Hermann," said Rolf, causing Hermann to jump in surprise. Rolf spoke with his mouth full, as he was gobbling fish from the pile Hermann had made for him.

Up above, the man with the sack was now looking down from the window. He had seen Hermann swallow the ring!

As Rolf continued wolfing his bits of fish, he and Hermann heard rapid footsteps. The two men came racing around from the back of the house carrying their sacks. They stopped short as they spotted the cats. Then they grinned broadly and began inching toward them.

"Nice kitty!" said one.

"Good kitty!" said the other.

We should state for the record here that cats do not understand human speech and vice-versa. That said, cats easily grasp the *tone* of what humans say, especially if it is said insincerely while grinning inappropriately. That always meant trouble.

"I must say they are acting strangely," observed Hermann.

"Most definitely," said Rolf, snatching one last fish bit as they backed warily away.

At that, the men charged toward them, pulling out large and nasty looking knives! Rolf and Hermann knew well what humans did to animals with knives.

"I would advise we run," said Rolf.

"Just so," said Hermann.

And they did.

These cats had been chased before (many times) so they had an extensive repertoire of evasive maneuvers. When escaping from anything other than hawks, which were in a different category entirely, they followed one of two tried-and-true systems. If the pursuer was about the same size as they, System One was used — zigzags, sudden turns, and unexpected double-backs. If the pursuer was larger, System Two was preferred, in which they ducked though any handy opening too small for the pursuer to fit. Either system might include climbing things, since nothing that chased cats could climb as well as a cat.

In a swift execution of System Two, they used a simple straight-away dash with a left feint followed by a sharp right turn that set up their finish — zipping effortlessly through a small gap under the backyard fence. In under five seconds they'd left the two humans far behind.

They were, however, mystified by the sudden attack, and they discussed this as they now casually strolled along. "Who do you suppose they were?" asked Hermann.

"I'm sure I don't know," said Rolf, "But then, humans all tend to look alike."

"True, true. But why were they so angry at us? Dressed as they were, they're obviously not friends of the people who live in that house."

Rolf nodded, pondered, and then said, "Perhaps one was the butcher from which we stole that excellent steak some days ago."

"Could be. Or they might have come from the house where we broke all those wine glasses in trying to get to the turkey on the dinner table."

"Possibly, possibly."

Hermann sighed at the memory, "I wish we'd gotten to that turkey."

"Ah!" said Rolf, "Perhaps they are the owners of the parakeet on which we dined Thursday a week."

"Good thought! I'd quite forgotten that!"

They were wrong on all counts. The two men were burglars. They had broken into the house of the Bichon Frise just after Rolf had entered and, among other things, they had stolen the diamond ring. They were very, very upset that Hermann had swallowed it, for it was the single most valuable thing they had stolen in their whole, albeit rather limited, careers.

The burglars' names were Acker and Eckhard. Acker, who had tripped over the dog, was short, thin and pale, with freckles and wispy red hair which clung to his forehead in damp curls. Eckhard was equally thin, but a head taller than his cohort. He had a black beard and bushy black brows that seemed forever knitted in a look of mild confusion.

While not the most quick-witted criminals in Dunkelhaven, they acted most quickly in this matter. They raced to a small rundown house on the very edge of town. Surrounded by a tall fence, it was the home of a devious friend of theirs. He made his living poaching in the local forests, which is to say, hunting animals he had no right to hunt.

To aid him in this illegal profession, he had a bloodhound. Her name was Annalise. Like Rolf and Hermann, she had grown up in rough circumstances. Her chocolate colored fur was dusty and matted, and always seemed to have a few burrs stuck in it. One ear was shorter than the other, due to a fight when she was a pup (she won). But she had an excellent nose and a great spirit, and she had always served her master faithfully.

As a result, said master wasn't about to sell her. He drove a hard bargain just to rent her. Acker and Eckhard argued that she should come cheap because she was only a female. The poacher claimed that she was a better tracker than most male hounds, which was true. At the end of the haggling, Acker and Eckhard angrily gave him all the valuables they had just stolen, buying Annalise's services for only as long as needed to catch the cats.

Annalise was quite surprised to find herself leashed and led away from the only home she had known since being taken from her mother. She knew that dogs sometimes were, for reasons unclear to animals, traded to other humans, so she assumed this is what had happened.

Straight away, Acker and Eckhard raced back to the fancy neighborhood. Annalise had heard of it, but had never seen it, and she was awed to see the great houses and broad shaded streets. Was this where her new masters lived? From the look of them, she didn't think so, but one could always hope. It made her think of the well-groomed dogs she often saw at the market where her former master sold his illegal wares. She admired them and wistfully wished that one day he might brush out her fur in that way. This had never happened, of course.

She was pulled from these thoughts when the men stopped at the tree where Hermann and Rolf had collected the smoked fish. Acker shoved her nose to the ground. It was obvious he wanted her to pick up a scent, but she was offended that he was so rough about it.

She immediately caught the desired scent, and was at first confused. Cats? They wanted her to hunt cats? That was odd, since humans did not eat or make clothes out of cats. Indeed, your average bloodhound would have been insulted at the command. But, as it happened, Annalise recognized the intertwined scents of Rolf and Hermann. This was significant because she thought of them as "The Hated Rolf and Hermann."

Here's why. Not only had she heard numerous stories of their sneaky exploits, she herself had once been tricked by them. The previous summer, Hermann had leapt her fence and come staggering toward her lowly dog house, hissing and frothing at the mouth. Convinced that the horrid cat was rabid, Annalise had dashed to find her owner, whimpering and cowering. Only then did she see Rolf leap in over the fence, snatch her evening meal, and leap back out. Hermann, suddenly "cured," was gone just as quickly. Adding injury to insult, her owner had kicked her for being fearful and annoying.

So, her new masters would have her hunt Rolf and Hermann, would they? Annalise set out on this trail with an eager howl!

CHAPTER TWO

By now far from the rich neighborhood and back to Dunkelhaven's more unsavory environs, Rolf and Hermann had quite forgotten about the mysterious knife-wielding humans. They were in search of something to drink after their excellent but salty lunch — something more tasty than water, of course.

To this end, they headed for a stop only recently added to their usual rounds. It was on a perpetually muddy alley bordered by dismal one room shacks. An old lady who lived in one of them had started setting out a saucer of milk once each day on the slanted board that served as her front porch. The first time they had noticed this, Rolf and Hermann had assumed she was offering it to them. However, when they had approached the milk, she had attacked them with a broom, forcing them to abandon that assumption. They soon discovered the real reason for her generosity; a new litter of five kittens had been born somewhere nearby.

So, Rolf and Hermann had needed an alternate approach to getting the milk, and they elected to use the same ploy used on Annalise. Hermann would stagger toward the old lady, performing his standard rabies act. She would run into her shack to hide. He and Rolf would then trot over to the milk saucer and drain it dry.

This was the fourth time they'd pulled this trick and, remarkably, it had worked again. Rolf and Hermann began happily lapping. As usually happened, the kittens appeared, tottering toward them, mewing annoyingly, hoping to get to the milk. But it was easy to scare them away, since they were frightened of everything.

As Rolf and Hermann were enjoying the last of the milk, they were feeling this day was among the best they'd had lately. Then they became aware of the mournful howl of a bloodhound.

"I hate bloodhounds," observed Rolf, licking his lips. "Don't dogs make enough stupid noises without that awful moaning?"

"I quite agree, Rolf," said Hermann. "Even that Bichon's yap is less annoying. And anyway, what's it moaning about here in town? This isn't some country hunting field."

"Unless we happen to see a mouse," laughed Rolf.

"Exactly," snickered Hermann as he scoured the saucer for the last traces of milk. Then he suddenly burped uncomfortably.

"Hermann, please!" Rolf remonstrated, because burping was very un-catlike.

"Terribly sorry, dear Rolf," said Hermann. "That last bit of fish I swallowed does not seem to have settled well."

"Well, if you had been paying attention to my whereabouts instead of mindlessly gobbling, perhaps —"

Rolf stopped because he realized that the howling was coming closer. They saw Annalise round a corner up the street.

"Oh, look," said Hermann, "It's the hound from whom we stole food last summer. Annalise, I think she's called."

"Ah yes," said Rolf. "I didn't like that hound. You remember the next time we tried the rabid-cat gambit, she nearly killed you?"

"Of course I remember," said Hermann. "I reserve an extra measure of dislike for any dog that a) tries to kill me and b) can be fooled only once." In Rolf and Hermann's experience, the typical dog could be fooled multiple times. Annalise had not proven typical. After that single escapade, they had had to strictly avoid her house when making their rounds.

Up to that moment, this was an everyday conversation in which they were only half interested. They became full-interested when Annalise, charging forward, looked right at them and howled, "I seeeeeeee youuuu-uuuuuu, hated Rolffff and Hermannnnnn!"

"The hound is hunting — *us?*" exclaimed Hermann.

"It would seem so!" said Rolf. "But — but why is she not leashed? Why is she not captive in her hovel of a yard?"

Now they saw Acker and Eckhard dashing around the corner, doing their best to keep up with Annalise. When the burglars saw Rolf and Hermann, their eyes lit up — and they pulled their knives!

"The knife-wielders!" cried Hermann.

"They're *still* after us?" asked alarmed Rolf rhetorically. This was unprecedented, since humans who chased cats usually forgot them in just a few minutes and didn't even seem to recognize them the next day. He followed his unanswered question with, "*Run!*"

This "Run!" was said with far more emphasis than the earlier one because, while escaping from humans was one thing, getting away from a dog, and a bloodhound no less, was an entirely different basket of smoked fish. It required reliance on escape System One, a much more energy-intensive and risky enterprise.

Rolf and Hermann bolted for their lives, streaking straight away from advancing Annalise and her murderous masters.

"What do we do? What do we do?" Hermann rasped as they ran. In times like this he relied on Rolf's quick thinking.

"Make some big jumps, get out of her sight, and double back!" ordered Rolf. "Follow me!"

He sprang from the street to a barrel. From the barrel to a stack of crates. From the crates to a shed roof. Hermann made the first two jumps, but failed to reach the shed roof. He fell!

"Rolf!" he yelped as, thud, he landed behind the crates.

Rolf knew from the sounds alone what had happened. He spun around and dashed back to the edge of the roof, making sure Annalise saw him. Then he dashed to the other side of the roof, out of view. As he hoped, the dog went around the shed to try to head him off, and missed seeing Hermann huddled behind the crates.

Hermann cowered and waited until Acker and Eckhard had also run blindly past him, then went back the way they had come. He knew that the more agile Rolf would do the same by some aerial route. Rolf was such a good leaper.

When Annalise reached the far side of the shed, neither cat was in view. She knew at once she'd been duped. Whirling about to retrace her steps, she angrily thought, *My, those cats are good!*

Hermann was almost all the way back to the old lady's shack when he spotted an old collapsed freight wagon leaning against a fence. There was a small opening allowing access underneath it, and under he went.

Rolf was already there. He was that fast.

The wagon lay at an angle against the fence, creating a long, dark triangular space. Time and debris had closed gaps so that the area was actually rather cozy, in a dank and musty way. Rolf and Hermann were safe for the moment. Rolf had made many grand leaps getting back here, and Annalise would have a hard time picking up his trail.

They panted, tongues lolling out in a most uncat-like way.

"What on *earth* is going on?" gasped Hermann.

"I'm sure I don't know," wheezed Rolf. "I've never seen humans so determined."

They both flinched as a shape came out of the darkness toward them; then relaxed when they saw it was just a scruffy female cat.

"Oh! You scared us," said Hermann.

"Did I?" she said, with an unsettling edge to the question. She was clearly not some human's pampered pet. Her dirty white fur was wild and frizzy, her tail long with a question mark arch, eyes quick. She was on the thin side, even emaciated, but under different circumstances both Rolf and Hermann might have found her exotically attractive. For now, Rolf just wanted her to keep quiet.

"Silence!" he commanded. "There's a bloodhound after us. We need to be quiet."

"A bloodhound? Why?"

"We don't know! I said be quiet!" Rolf expected his commands to be obeyed.

But the female kept talking. "A bloodhound chasing two cats? Right in town?"

"Madame," pleaded Hermann, "could we perhaps go over the details when the situation is not quite so tense?"

But the female went right on, her hostile eyes narrowing, "Would that be the two cats who steal milk from kittens?"

"What?" said Hermann.

"What? said Rolf.

Then they paled as they saw five little kittens toddle out of the shadows behind her. Thin, wan, big-eyed, hungry little kittens. She was the mother of the new litter!

She raised one paw, pointed it at them, and unleashed a caterwauling screech like an animal possessed, "They're in heeeeeeere!"

Annalise heard it. A dog on the moon could have heard it. And in the next second Rolf and Hermann heard her answering howl coming toward them.

They dashed frantically out through the little hole, only to find the hound already bearing down on them. As they raced down the street, Hermann literally felt her wet breath on his rump. Annalise could not help her slight tendency to drool when excited. She was, after all, a bloodhound. It served as a significant motivator, for Hermann managed to keep pace even with wiry Rolf, and they both stayed ahead of the dog.

But they could not run forever. They needed an escape plan. Rolf led the way — toward the docks of Dunkelhaven's small harbor on the river. They were running too hard to spare breath for speech, but Hermann guessed he knew what the plan was. It was that most detested of variations on System One escapes, to be used only in the most desperate situations.

Rolf shot out onto one of the docks. It was rather busy on that day, because a Dutch sea-going freighter, the Eagle, was anchored in the harbor and workers were unloading her cargo. The Weser River provided excellent access to the North Sea, and forward-thinking businessmen of Dunkelhaven, like those in many towns along the river, had built the harbor seeking to establish their town as a port for world trade.

On this day, however, Rolf and Hermann did much to upset that dream. Zigging and zagging among the startled workers, they caused them to drop crates, bales, and boxes. Two men lost control of an immense hogshead of ale they were rolling along the dock. The barrel crashed into a mooring post and its bung popped out. Instantly a huge beer fountain erupted, drenching the whole area in a sticky, but rather good-tasting rain. The Eagle's captain would later note in his log, unfairly, that he found the Dunkelhaven dock workers to be sloppy and prone to drinking on the job.

The barrel mishap did buy Rolf and Hermann some precious seconds on Annalise, because she skidded in the slippery beer and crashed headlong into the barrel. They had to love that dogs, in their enthusiasm, skidded so much.

Meanwhile, the cats were coming to the end of the dock. Hermann knew he'd guessed right. Rolf's plan *was* the most detested escape. Without slowing, he and Rolf rocketed off the dock, sailing out into empty air, graceful feline shapes in perfect form — only to plummet inevitably down, down, down — into, into, into —

THE WATER!

With a deafening splash the despised liquid filled their ears and blinded their eyes. They felt the awful stuff rush into their fur like some hungry parasite, matting it, flattening it, turning their coats into slimy, leaden cloaks that threatened to pull them under.

They flailed with their paws, claws useless against the frothing wetness, as they performed that most embarrassing of acts, the Dog Paddle. Embarrassment aside, cats can swim rather well when they absolutely have to, and they made steady headway.

They dared a glance back. Annalise was loping frenetically back and forth along the edge of the dock. Acker and Eckhard joined her, but stopped. They cursed and brandished their knives, but were unwilling to plunge into the harbor after the cats. The truth: neither could swim.

Acker swatted Annalise, "Fool dog!" She cowered and tucked her tail, for she felt the failure to catch the cats at least as keenly than he. Acker was about to hit her again when Eckhard stayed his hand.

"Stop it. She found 'em in jig time, didn't she? She'll find 'em again."

Acker mumbled something that indicated grudging agreement, and the duo stalked back up the dock. As Annalise followed, she was deep in thought. An extraordinary thing had happened on this chase. That mother cat had deliberately told her where Rolf and Hermann were. She was quite sure nothing like that had ever happened before in the history of dog-cat chases. But what did it mean?

Across the harbor, after much dog paddling, bedraggled Rolf and Hermann hauled themselves out onto the far shore.

"Most unpleasant," said Hermann, his normally silky fur drooping from his cheeks in drippy Halloween pin curls.

"Exceptionally so," said Rolf, his flattened coat giving him the look of a charcoal stick figure. "But, once again, we have prevailed!"

"We have! Due in no small measure to your unparalleled quick-wittedness. My thanks to you, as always."

"You are welcome, as always." Rolf then thought for a moment, listening to the annoying drip of water from his tail, and added, "I suggest, however, that we repair to the Most Secret Place, lest those beastly humans see fit to continue the chase."

"Let us repair at once," nodded Hermann.

Only rarely had Rolf and Hermann felt the need to hide in the Most Secret Place. The last time was during the invasion of the wild cat. This insufferable, frizzy-haired, smelly creature had come stalking out of the forest after a particularly hard winter, and had promptly taken over Rolf and Hermann's preferred food outlets. An attempt to stand up to him had resulted in a disastrous fight and a narrow escape. They had feared they might have to live in the Most Secret Place indefinitely. But soon the wild cat, unwise in the ways and dangers of humans, attempted a bold steak theft at the butcher shop — in broad daylight, mind you — and met a very graphic end which we will not detail, other than to say it was one reason Rolf and Hermann knew well what humans could do with knives.

The Most Secret Place was the church bell tower, which dominated the town square. It was not easy to get all the way up to the tower, even for a cat. That was, of course, what made it a good place. One had to climb a walnut tree, vault from it to the end of one of the church's flying buttresses and tiptoe along the buttress' stone arch to the roof. Next, one went along the peak of the roof to the tower, which could only be climbed by leaping very carefully up a series of gargoyles. But all this could be done. And they did it.

The sun was setting. Their fur was dry enough to begin getting it licked into decent shape. As they went comfortably to work on this task, they heard soft rustling above them. It was nothing unusual; just the local bats awakening for their night's feasting on flying insects. Soon they would start fluttering about, making their irritating beep noises like miniature airborne submarines.

Except the bats did not fly off. Instead, they joined their beep voices together in a high-pitched, grating chorus, "Th-ey're he-e-e-e-r-e! Rolf-and-Herman-are-up-h-e-e-e-e-r-e!"

Rolf and Hermann hissed and spat and leapt up the walls, but there was no way to reach the bats' upside-down perches.

"Quiet! Quiet, you repugnant little demons!" demanded exasperated Rolf. But the little demons went right on beeping.

"This is madness!" Rolf declared. "That spiteful female cat may have incorrectly thought we'd wronged her, but now we are betrayed by *bats*? Why?! What possible interest have they in us, or in the hound and her despised humans?"

Hermann took all of Rolf's questions seriously, even rhetorical ones. So he thought, then offered, "Well, dear Rolf, it is true that last winter we ate that older bat who fell from his perch while asleep."

"And I was sorry we did! He wasn't even that good."

"Even so, your opinion, however valid, may be moot in this situation." Hermann was correct. Bats, it turns out, hold grudges. Annalise's howls earlier in the day had alerted them that she was pursuing "The Hated Rolf and Hermann," so the bats had decided to aid her in that goal.

At that moment, Annalise, Acker and Eckhard were half way across town. Try as she might, Annalise had been unable to pick up Rolf and Hermann's scent. When she heard the distant shriek of the bats, it was at least as surprising as the betrayal of Rolf and Hermann by the mother cat, but she wasn't about to deny her good fortune. With a howl to tell her masters she was again on the trail, she dashed toward the town square.

The cats cringed as they heard Annalise's call. Rolf sprang to the top of the church bell and scanned the surroundings. Sure enough, there was Annalise, racing toward the church. She spotted Rolf and howled in triumph. Right behind her came Acker and Eckhard.

Rolf jumped back down, quite rattled, "It's them! They've *still* not forgotten us!"

They had no choice but to flee, for they had often observed that any human was welcome in this particular building and they knew that, therefore, Acker and Eckhard would be welcome, and would soon find their way to the bell tower.

They fled down the gargoyles and along the roof, Rolf choosing a route hidden from Annalise's view. Not daring to delay, they leapt clear to the ground from the end of a flying buttress. It meant for a painful landing, but they scrambled up and sped off into the darkness. It would take Annalise some time to realize they were gone, circle the church, and pick up their trail.

They sprinted across town, taking to trees and fence tops to foil Annalise's nose, then made another perilous climb to the Next Most Secret Place. It was the flat roof of the Millers Guild. Unlike the church tower, it had no protection from the elements, but at least it could not be seen from any of the shorter buildings nearby, and the cats knew for sure they were completely invisible from the ground.

Back at the church, Annalise had quickly found where the cats jumped down, but just as quickly lost them at the base of the first tree they had climbed. She realized she'd been outfoxed by the elusive cats again!

As she circled, trying to find the trail, Acker snarled, "She's lost them again!"

"Give her a moment," admonished Eckhard.

Annalise certainly needed a moment, for she was thinking very hard. On the one paw, she was faced with cats whose escape skills outmatched those of any animal she'd ever pursued. On the other paw, there were these remarkable announcements of the cats' whereabouts. On a third paw, she was well aware that her new masters were angry and impatient. They seemed even more impatient than her previous master, and that was saying something. Regardless, more than anything, a good dog hated disappointing a master. And Annalise was a very good dog.

From all these thoughts sprang a radical idea. She theorized that she had an opportunity to do something that might not only be the key to catching her prey, but also be quite extraordinary in its own right.

Impulsively deciding to gamble on her theory, she dashed ahead of Acker and Eckhard, deliberately gaining a long distance. She knew that the first part of her plan would probably anger them even more, and she needed time.

She zigged down one cobblestone street, zagged down another, and soon spotted her goal, a group of garbage pigs working a fresh pile. She singled out a youngish one and approached him, keeping ears and tail down so as not to appear aggressive.

"Say there, pig," she said, "Do you happen to know of the cats Rolf and Hermann?"

The pig eyed her suspiciously. It was odd for a dog to talk to a pig. She knew this, but hoped he would overlook it. After a bit more suspicious eyeing, he did, "Of course I know of them. Why, only a fortnight past they hoodwinked me out of a particularly delectable piece of nearly fresh fish, much to my frustration." Contrary to what you may think, pigs are very smart and quite well spoken. "And," he added huffily, "my name is Beauregard."

"Well, I have a proposal for you, Beauregard" said Annalise.

"A proposal from a bloodhound to a pig? What have we in common?" asked Beauregard even more huffily.

"More than you may think," said Annalise slyly.

Meanwhile, on the next street over, Acker and Eckhard trudged along, looking everywhere, unsure which direction Annalise had gone.

"Fool hound! Why does she not sound?" railed Acker, annoyed that she was not howling to give them her location.

"She'll sound when she's caught the scent again. I must say you are fair impatient in this matter, Acker."

"Impatient am I? Impatient! Does it not worry you that what goes in a cat's mouth eventually passes out the other end?"

Eckhard took a few steps before his eyebrows suddenly knitted from standard-confused to deeply-concerned, "Blazes! I'd not thought of that!

How long before the cat does that unhappy thing?"

"How should I know!? I know nothing of cat time tables! But I know enough to worry!"

At that moment, they turned a corner and spotted Annalise. But the sight did not make Acker any happier.

"A pig! She's cornered herself a *pig*!?" He charged forward.

Annalise had just finished her proposal when she heard Acker's angry footsteps behind her. She had long ago learned to recognize the sound of the special skip-step a human must take to prepare a kick. Almost without thinking, she sprang deftly sideways. Acker missed his kick, and his leg went up with such force he flew up and fell heavily on his butt, right in the garbage. The pigs scattered, grunting with annoyance.

He jumped to his feet, even more furious, but Annalise immediately put her nose to the street and raced away with a howl, pretending to be hard on the trail of the cats.

"Stay your anger, Acker," said Eckhard. "See there, she's on the hunt again."

Across town, on the roof of the Miller's Guild, Rolf and Hermann were finally starting to relax. They'd been momentarily startled when a group of pigeons landed on the far side of the roof, but the birds were only settling in for the night and had gone right to sleep.

Rolf and Hermann did not notice, a moment later, a house sparrow who landed next to the dozing pigeons and briefly whispered something to them.

They *did* notice what happened next. The pigeons started in cooing. And it wasn't the nice coo-coo sound pigeons normally make. As with the bats, it was a shockingly loud atonal symphony: "Thoor Hooore! Thoor Hooore! Roolf and Hooorman oor oop hooore!" Yes, pigeons have an odd accent.

In seconds, Annalise's howl was again heard in the distance. And, again, there was no choice but to flee.

We won't go into all the details of the next harrowing twenty-four hours, because the same basic steps were repeated over and over. It seemed that every animal who saw Rolf and Hermann — mammal, fish, fowl or amphibian — was happy to betray their whereabouts to Annalise.

When the duo hid in the attics of abandoned buildings, the mice turned them in. When they hid behind a mountain of scent-masking manure outside one of the stables, the horses turned them in. When they hid in that marshy area of the city park where almost nobody ever went, the *frogs* turned them in!

While this was utterly inexplicable to Rolf and Hermann, it wasn't really without explanation. You see, to be fair to all these seemingly traitorous animals, Rolf and Hermann had, at one time or another, lied to, tricked, bamboozled, blind-sided, flummoxed, one-upped, double-crossed, tripped-up, side-stepped, screwed over or eaten one of them. Except the pigeons, but the pigeons had observed these other acts from their lofty vantage points. Oh, and Rolf and Hermann had never eaten a frog, either, but with frogs they just couldn't resist playing chase-and-hold, chase-and-hold, chase-and-hold. It was a great pastime in one's off hours but, of course, really upsetting to frogs.

To take Rolf and Hermann's side, they felt that their approach to life was simply the natural way of things. It was "survival of the fittest." It was "to the strong (and/or smart; and/or cute) go the spoils." It was "the early bird catches the worm unless a cat is hiding nearby."

But the sad fact was everyone hated them, and Annalise had taken advantage of it by simply asking the garbage pigs to spread the word that she was after them. Her plan had exceeded her wildest hopes. She now had virtually every creature in Dunkelhaven helping her — an animal internet the likes of which had never been seen before.

It meant the cats had flat run out of luck. There was no place they could hide. This took a grim toll on their nerves, their sleep, and their stomachs. Especially their stomachs. Never had they gone so long without their dear friend, food. And so, they were forced to consider a course of action that they had never considered before; to act upon that earlier suggestion of Rolf's — to leave Dunkelhaven forever.

But even this was not easily done. There were only two ways to leave the town. One was to sneak aboard the weekly coach that took humans from Dunkelhaven to the next nearest town, many miles distant. The other was to sneak aboard the freighter in the harbor that was bound for who knew where.

There was, of course, a third way: simply to disappear into the forest that surrounded the town. And for a brief moment, Rolf and Hermann paused on a rooftop to contemplate that dark foreboding wall of trees. But it was known to hold wolves, hawks, vultures, owls, vipers, Eurasian lynx — and wild cats like the Neanderthal they'd encountered earlier.

So the forest option was quickly dismissed, Rolf declaring, "Unacceptable. We are civilized cats. Upper crust. Elite. *Haut monde.*"

"Oh yes!" agreed Herman, "the most *monde.*"

Therefore, late in the afternoon, they tried the coach. They took a long time circling the main stop in the town square, watching for opportunities to slip aboard. But when they at last made their move, leaping up and ducking behind luggage on the roof, they were spotted immediately by the surprisingly quick and surprisingly angry coachman, who instantly snatched them in either hand and flung them headlong to a rough and ungraceful landing.

That left only the freighter, the Eagle. Back they slunk toward the harbor they so recently had swum. Though not a great distance, it was no easy journey, for it had to be accomplished avoiding all other animals. They leapt from roof top to roof top. They wriggled under porches and hedges. They slogged miserably through muddy ditches rather than risk being spotted on bridges. But at last they were hidden in the center of a hawser coiled on the dock. From there they studied the sailing vessel.

Ships caused a lot of discussion among animals, who liked to gossip about where these mysterious "moving houses" came from and where they went. Birds had followed them for many miles, as far as the North Sea, only to find that they kept on going until they completely disappeared beyond the edge of the ocean. Even sea gulls didn't know where the ships went.

This did not matter to Rolf and Hermann. They knew any ship must eventually go to other human habitats, and they wanted out now!

Having unloaded the Eagle the day before, the dockworkers were today busily loading her with new cargo. Some men lugged crates and barrels up her springy gangplank. Others swung nets full of cargo aboard using a crane that was powered by still other men walking back and forth inside large wooden wheels because, you've probably guessed, no one had invented motors yet.

Rolf and Hermann saw no way they could sneak up the narrow gangplank undetected. So it was the crane and cargo net on which they focused. For each load, the net was first lowered and laid flat on the dock. Men tumbled barrels and crates onto it. Then the edges of the net were raised and it became a sort of oversized grocery bag that the crane then lifted aboard the ship. After watching this process twice more, Rolf and Hermann inched forward and stationed themselves behind a mooring cleat. Its squat "T" shape made it ideal for tying up boats and equally ideal for hiding cats.

The next time the loaded net was raised, Rolf and Hermann sprang onto it. Their claws stuck like kitty Velcro, and up they went as the net was swung aboard. Luckily for the cats, it was lowered straight through a hatch into the dark hold. There, the men waiting to unload the net never saw the two silent cat-shapes leap off and scamper toward the bow, hiding among the already-stowed cargo.

"Not spotted by a single human!" enthused Hermann.

"Not one!" said Rolf. "And I defy that evil Annalise to track us here! We shall ride in comfort and safety to a new home, dear Hermann!"

"A new home!" echoed Hermann excitedly.

Then they heard a sound. It came from behind them, in the total darkness toward the bow.

It was a soft unpleasant scratching; the kind of scratching that is made by furtive scuttling. Rolf and Hermann's ears rotated and their fur rose in unison because, as a general rule, cats don't like things that scuttle. Neither do most of the rest of us, for that matter.

"That is not a human-made sound," whispered Hermann.

"No, it is not," said Rolf.

They widened their eyes for maximum light gathering, staring into the blackness. And in a moment they were able to pick out grotesque humpbutt shapes inching toward them — over cargo, under ropes, along beams.

Rats.

Now normally rats avoid cats and cats avoid rats. Even though rats are technically smaller, they're kind of evenly matched in the furiously-fierce-fighting department. So, by unspoken agreement, each species prefers to go its own way.

Please understand, cats are not *afraid* of rats. However, these were bilge rats. Rats the like of which Rolf and Hermann had never *ever* seen. These rats didn't avoid cats. They didn't avoid anything but humans. Any unlucky critter that entered their dark, mildewed domain was an invader to be repelled — or eaten.

Rolf and Hermann's eyes adjusted further to the darkness, but this only meant they now saw details they'd rather not. The vermin were demonic! Mangy, riddled with sores from untold flea bites, scarred by untold battles — and very smelly. The rats bared gnarled, yellow-stained fangs below their maniacal blood-shot eyes.

"They're *huge!*" whispered Hermann in total horror. Actually they just looked huge. When you're scared, a rat looks, on average, 2.5 times its normal size. It's just a power they have, even over cats. Their true size notwithstanding, however, the rats now charged the hapless duo.

As noted above, a cat will think twice before tackling a rat. Rolf and Hermann only had to think once to decide how to deal with an entire horde of bilge rats.

They ran. All-out. Full tilt.

They skimmed across the piled cargo, hurtled out the open hatch and down the ship's gangplank, weaving and dodging among the dockworkers' legs, causing untold amounts of cargo to be dropped. Crates cracked! Barrels burst! Trunks tumbled overboard! Sacks were soaked! The Eagle's captain made another negative entry about Dunkelhaven in his log!

Rolf and Hermann managed to reach their original hiding place on the dock, inside the coiled rope. After a moment, Hermann commented, "Rats are ugly on a good day. I never dreamed they could be as bad as those things!"

"Nor I, dear Hermann," said Rolf.

Night was falling. They stayed there for a long time, very disconsolate, for truly they had no where else to go. They didn't get to stay as long as they wanted, however, for they again heard the hated haunting hunting howl of Annalise. Some ridiculously small shrews who nested under the dock had spotted them. They relayed the news to a stray dog and, well, you get the point: the animal network had flashed the message straight to the bloodhound.

Rolf and Hermann peeked over the top of the rope. There she was in the distance, racing toward the docks, nose to the ground, tail in the air.

"We are lost!" moaned Hermann.

"Never say die," ordered Rolf, looking around. "Come!"

Rolf had a new plan. It was almost as extreme as the Most Hated Escape.

He led Hermann toward an area just upriver from the town. You remember that the rich people on the hill paid poor people to take their garbage someplace? Well, the poor people took it here, to a random area that today we'd call the city dump, so you could say that Dunkelhaven was rather ahead of its time in this regard. The local animals called it The Place of Ghastly Smells. Without plastic bags, bulldozers and such, everything was just right out there in the open — rotting.

Which was precisely why Rolf was heading there now.

"Where are we going?" panted Hermann.

"To the Place of Ghastly Smells."

"You can't be serious!" cried Hermann.

"If I'm not, you *can* say die, my dear Hermann," said Rolf grimly.

"But — why, dear Rolf? The Place of Ghastly Smells is so — so ghastly!"

"Yes, and it is therefore just the place where a certain insufferable dog might not be able to do what?"

Hermann thought, then brightened, "Where she might not be able to pick out *our* dainty cat aroma from the myriad and ghastly others?"

"Precisely, dear Hermann. So, breathe through your mouth — and follow!"

As night fell, Rolf and Hermann plunged bravely — well, if not bravely, at least desperately — into the town dump. It was, we remind you, spring. The long winter's build-up of tossed effluvia was now warming up for some serious decay. Flies swarmed. Maggots wriggled. Beetles infested. Fungus spread. And *everything* smelled with an intensity hard to imagine if you're a human, let alone a cat with a half way decent nose.

Rolf and Hermann picked their way through the stenchiferous landscape, Rolf on the lookout for a suitable hiding place, certain that Annalise, no matter how diligent, could not follow them. And indeed, at that moment, she was desperately searching the outer edge of the dump, having lost their trail.

Rolf spotted an enormous hollow tree which had fallen in some past century. He led Hermann inside and they followed its tortured, though at least less smelly, chambers.

"Here we shall wait, for a good and long time," announced Rolf. "Let Annalise lead her humans in circles until she drops!"

"But hopefully it is not so good and long a time that I drop before she does," said Hermann. "I am so hungry."

"As am I, dear Hermann. As am I. Now rest, rest."

As cats do when preparing to rest, they turned in circles, sniffed certain spots, and lay down. But they'd hardly set chin to paw when they heard an evil snickering, "Hi-heh, hi-heh, hi-heh."

Hermann shrank up against Rolf, whispering, "What is it?" Rolf didn't answer because he didn't want to admit he didn't know.

The snickering came from above them. They looked up to see, looking down on them, an enormously fat pack rat.

Now, pack rats, as you know, are not indigenous to Europe. They are native, rather, to the Americas. How this particular individual had made the long journey from there to this country eventually-to-be-called Germany is beyond the scope of this report, except to say that he had done so by stowing away on various ships. Since arriving in Dunkelhaven, he had built an appropriately enormous pack rat nest in the convoluted network of the great old tree's rotted roots.

"Is it a rat?" asked Hermann in a whisper.

"I think so," said Rolf.

"But it has a furry tail," argued Hermann. In fact, pack rats do have furry, rather than naked tails, giving them a very slight edge in the cute department. Meanwhile, the rat spoke, immediately clearing up the confusion over its species.

"Cats?" he chuckled. "Cats come visiting to home of rat?"

"Watch your tongue," hissed Rolf. "Or I'll spring up there and eat your head." Having just met with bilge rats, he didn't view this fat character as very dangerous.

"Might, might," giggled the rat. "Too, I might slip up my escape tunnels, and there call out to a certain bloodhound —"

"Don't!" yelped Hermann.

"Shh!" Rolf admonished Hermann. Then he said to the rat, in a friendlier tone, "No need for that. We're just — exploring. Curious cats. You know."

"Hi-heh, hi-heh, hi-heh," snickered the rat, sarcastically. "Yes. Exploring the Place of Ghastly Smells? Lovely place for delicate clean cats. Hi-heh."

"We'll just be on our way," said Rolf, fighting to control his temper. He started back along the hollow tree tunnel. Hermann slunk close behind him.

"Cats seek to board ship now in harbor," said the rat.

They stopped and looked over their shoulders at him. How could he know that?

He spoke before they could voice the question, "How could rat know that, cats ask?"

They nodded in cat unison.

"I trade with bilge rats of all ships. I give Dunkelhaven's finest foods. They bring fabulous collectibles from around the world."

He waddled to one side so that Rolf and Hermann could see further into his nest. Indeed, it was absolutely jammed with the most unusual odds and ends. Small tikis from Hawaii, coins from China, trinkets from Africa; on and on. There were also twigs, acorns, pine needles, rotting cloth, and a bent fork. Pack rats collect *every*thing. In truth, they are not so much collectors as hoarders.

"What do you do with all this stuff?" asked Hermann.

"I *have* it," replied the rat, proudly.

"Ah, I see," said Hermann, but didn't at all.

While the fastidious Rolf and Hermann were not impressed by the rat's disorderly collection, they were impressed by what he said next, "Ship in harbor next goes very far. To land called Pago-Pago, a place that has no winter *and*," he paused for effect, "where animals, especially cats, find great respect and kindness."

"How do you know such things?" demanded Rolf.

"Have been there," said the rat. This was true. He was an extremely well-traveled rat. While he was probably exaggerating about nice-to-animals part, he was being honest about the no-winter part.

He concluded grandly, in his smug way, "If cats did wish it, pack rat could maybe persuade bilge rats to let you board ship safe."

Very much wishing that, but not wanting to admit it, Rolf and Hermann turned fully around and faced him again.

"And why would pack rat do that for cats?" asked Rolf, pointedly mimicking the rat's odd verbal cadence.

"Something in Dunkelhaven pack rat has wished to have, but does not have. If cats bring it me, bilge rats might be persuaded."

"What is he saying?" whispered Hermann. "I think it's good, but I'm not sure."

Rolf decided to explain to Hermann later, and spoke instead to the pack rat, "What is it that you want, that you have wished to have?"

"Tick-tock, tick-tock" said the rat.

"Speak clearly!" snarled Rolf, inching forward.

The pack rat, much swifter than he looked, scurried to the rear of his nest and poised on tip-toe near one of his escape exits.

"Shall I go up? Shall I — call out?" he grinned through his huge, curved front teeth.

"No! No!" squeaked Hermann.

Rolf fought down his anger and humiliation. It was hard being civil to a rat, even one with a furry tail. "I simply mean, s-i-ir," he said, gagging on the "sir", "I do not yet understand that to which you refer."

"Tick-tock, tick-tock. Gold and shiny and round and beautiful — and ticking."

"Oh!" blurted Hermann, "Those round shiny things rich humans carry that constantly go cltch-cltch-cltch-cltch!"

The pack rat nodded and grinned again, "Tick-tock!" He was referring, of course, to a pocket watch. Animals didn't know what they were for, but they knew that humans carried them around and looked at them often, seemingly with admiration.

"All right, we'll find a tick-tock," said Rolf, "and when we do, you promise you will —?"

"Not any tick-tock will do!" interrupted the rat. "One and one only. One I have seen on dark nights, in dark places, where I meander and collect. It is carried by a tall thin male human who rides in a black carriage. You will know it by this sign."

From under a corner of his pile of demented detritus he tugged a white linen handkerchief. This he dangled so the cats could see the embroidered monogram. It was a bold, black letter "F" bordered by elaborate red filigree.

"This same picture is on the door of the human's carriage. Find him! Look for him in darkness, for that is when he travels. Follow him! Get for me his lovely tick-tock! But I tell you this warning, too. Bilge rats say to me they can tell by loaded cargo their ship sails soon, maybe in two-three days. That time only is all you have. When ship's bell begins to ring, this tells the humans the ship is ready. Soon after that, ship is gone, gone."

CHAPTER THREE

Rolf and Hermann agreed to steal the specific watch requested, albeit with grave misgivings about making a bargain with a rodent. In return, the pack rat would speak to the bilge rats, convincing them to let the cats board the Eagle without being eaten.

Their only other option was to remain in the Place of Ghastly Smells indefinitely, with no guarantee that Annalise's spies might not lead her there. So, they went back out that very night, a yellow moon creeping skyward to light their way. Slinking and cat-tip-toeing, they made another traumatic journey across town, scrupulously avoiding every living thing.

They arrived at the place where the rat said he had last seen the man. It was one of those places where humans drank drinks of various colors, smoked burning weeds and sang and danced to very loud music. In Germany it was called a *bierwirtschaft*. We'd call it a bar or saloon. The animals called it a House of Humans Acting Stupid.

Generally, such places were to be avoided, because humans acting stupid often lashed out at animals unexpectedly. So Rolf and Hermann weren't thrilled about going there. However, when they arrived, they were heartened to discover a black carriage standing right in front of the place, its coachman waiting with the horses. They sneaked closer. In the flickering light of the lanterns on the porch, they saw that the coach had an elaborate "F" painted on each door that matched the one on the handkerchief perfectly!

"Good fortune at last smiles on us, Rolf," posited Hermann hopefully, as they slipped into a nice dark shadow across the street and waited.

Rolf just grunted, "Perhaps." He had been brooding since they left the dump. "We have sunk to this, Hermann. Cats working for a rat!"

"Ah, well, from that perspective it is indeed a sorry state of affairs," nodded Hermann. "Still, these are extraordinary circumstances, betrayed as we are by every animal in town."

"He should be food!" growled Rolf. "I've a mind to go right back there and —!"

"Wait!" whispered Hermann, "Look."

A tall thin man had come out of the *bierwirtschaft*. With pointed chin, angular nose and close-cropped, black wavy hair, he moved in sudden bursts, quick and precise. He wore a black, high-cut tail coat with huge, flared lapels and white silk neck cloth tied in the popular hunting style. Completing his look were tight-fitting trousers and black boots which rose almost to his knees. In other words, he was the height of high fashion. He also carried a heavy black lacquered cane. He spoke in a low voice to the coachman, and climbed into the carriage.

Hermann was excited, "'Tall and thin!' The pack rat said a tall and thin human! That must be him! The human with the tick-tock!"

"Yes. We shall stalk him relentlessly until we find where he keeps it!"

Rolf and Hermann shot forward and sprang silently up onto the rear of the carriage. Another leap took them to the empty luggage rack on top.

"Good fortune, again," offered Hermann, who really did try to take a cheerier view than Rolf.

"How so?" harrumphed Rolf

"Well, riding on this carriage will make it almost impossible for Annalise to pick up our scent."

So obsessed had he been with the rat bargain, Rolf hadn't thought of that. He elevated his chin in a half nod of agreement. Such affirmation from Rolf, however slight, always made Hermann smile.

They nestled down side by side and relaxed for the first time in many hours, happy to go wherever the carriage was headed. They did not know they would not feel relaxed again for quite some time.

The carriage wound through the dark streets, the horses' hooves clipping and clopping, the iron-rimmed wheels occasionally screeching on the cobblestones. But soon the screeching gave way to the softer rustle of the dirt road outside of town. The carriage kept moving into the countryside for some time until it suddenly lurched to a stop. Rolf and Hermann sat up, on the alert.

They were at the intersection of the main road and a rough side trail. The tall man got quickly out. "Go on!" he ordered his coachman. The man slapped the reins, turned the horses, and headed back toward town. Rolf and Hermann waited until the carriage passed behind a tree, then leapt down and slunk back to where the tall man stood. He was clearly nervous and agitated.

"Why has he gotten off his nice comfortable carriage in the middle of nowhere?" whispered Hermann.

Rolf just shook his head. It was quite strange. Normally, humans were more predictable.

The man opened his tail coat and tugged on a silver watch fob dangling from his waistcoat. Rolf and Hermann had no interest in the fob, but you may be interested to know that it was custom made in the shape of a stylized lightning bolt, certainly unusual for the time.

Anyway, he tugged on the silver lightning bolt and out slid his watch, attached to the fob by a delicate gold chain. As the watch dangled and swayed enticingly, cat ears perked up. They could hear it ticking even from fifty feet away.

"There it is!" cried Rolf.

"Yes, yes! Our good luck continues!" exclaimed Hermann. As noted elsewhere, this was not good luck, but it is understandable that Rolf and Hermann didn't realize it.

The man opened the watch and held it up in the moonlight. As he turned it about, trying to catch the light, the watch gleamed and sparkled beautifully. Rolf and Hermann could see how the easily impressed pack rat would covet it.

Having read the time, he snapped it shut and began to pace back and forth. Waiting. For what?

Their heads turned in unison as they heard hoof beats and a soft clattering. A rude and battered two-wheeled cart approached along the rutted side trail that joined the main road. The cart was drawn by a lumbering old mule with one blind white eye.

A young man drove the cart, bouncing uncomfortably on its stiff wooden seat. He was rather handsome, but that was not something cats would notice. Behind him was a long wooden box, so long it hung off the back of the rickety little cart.

He pulled the mule to a stop and nodded humbly to the impatient thin man, "Sorry to be late, Doctor Frankenstein."

"Never mind, Fritz. Much to do," said the thin man, as he climbed aboard the cart. The young man named Fritz pulled the mule around they headed back up the trail.

Rolf and Hermann, of course, did not know the name Frankenstein. But you may have heard it once or twice. Please be aware that, a few years after these events, a young woman named Mary something, pretending to the title of "novelist," wrote a different and much embellished version of the story. Since then there have been about a billion books, movies, plays and comics based on it. Ours is the true account. Trust us. Oh, and while we're being truthful, Frankenstein wasn't really a doctor. He never finished his schooling. But he felt he was a genius anyway, so he insisted on being called "doctor." The local folk went along with it, because he was also rich.

Anyway, as the cats began following Doctor Frankenstein and Fritz, Rolf formulated plans. "When they stop, wherever they stop, you will rush up to the thin man and commence your rabid cat impersonation. He will jump back away from you. I will jump on him, grab the chain, yank out the watch, and we're off for Pago-Pago!"

"Bravo, Rolf!" said Hermann. And he began licking his lips to work up good "rabies" foam.

But Rolf's plan had to wait, for they had to follow the cart a long way. This was surprising and frustrating. In those days, it was very odd for humans to go traipsing around in darkness. A low fog rolled across the land, making their whiskers tingle with condensation.

Finally, the cart topped a hill, and the cats realized where it was headed — The Dunkelhaven cemetery. Gravestones poked up through the fog like spectral islands.

Herman's eyes became large and round, "Rolf! It's that place where the humans take their dead!" he gasped expositionally.

"Shh!" hissed Rolf, though he was unnerved, too. Cats don't like hanging around dead things. That's a job for vultures — and bugs — and maybe certain dogs.

Fritz stopped the cart next to a fresh grave. The cats settled behind a gravestone, watching the humans intently. "Be ready," ordered Rolf

But the smell of that fresh earth stirred something in Hermann, "Rolf, please excuse me. But first, I think I must do some kitty business," he whispered.

"Then do it! Just do it quietly!" snapped Rolf. Hermann slipped behind a second gravestone.

Fritz and Doctor Frankenstein climbed down from the cart, grabbed shovels from the back, and began earnestly digging away the damp earth of the grave.

As Rolf kept watching, Hermann suddenly rejoined him, "I couldn't do it. I seem to be rather plugged up. I think it's that bad fish I swallowed."

"Hermann, please! We have more important matters!"

"But I'm uncomfortable!"

"You will be more so if we don't get that tick-tock and get on that ship!" Rolf's gaze remained fixed on the two digging men.

Hermann turned his attention to them also, wondering, "They don't have a dead human with them. Why are they digging?"

"I'm sure I don't know," said Rolf. "But it's no matter. To the task at hand! Ready your thespian skills!"

Hermann nodded. Licking his lips to get his foam on again, he stepped from behind the gravestone and staggered toward Doctor Frankenstein and Fritz, hissing and spitting all the way.

Doctor Frankenstein saw him first. But, unlike most humans treated to Hermann's display, he did not flinch. He did not blanch. Indeed, he barely blinked as he instantly *swung his shovel with deadly force!*

While Hermann was not as fast as Rolf in mind or in body, when real danger threatened, he nevertheless could be quick. He sling-shot himself sideways, and the shovel sliced six inches into the wet clay where he had stood.

Meanwhile, Fritz glanced up. "What was that?" he asked the doctor.

"Just a rabid cat."

"Hmm. The rabies seems to be prevalent this spring."

"Yes. Perhaps I should work on a cure for it. But only when we're done with the current project."

"Of course."

"Keep digging."

"Of course."

Back behind the gravestone, indignant Hermann rejoined Rolf.

"He tried to *kill* me!"

"Most inhospitable."

"You try it."

"Try what?"

"*You* go out and frighten him. *I'll* grab the watch."

"It's too late," said Rolf quickly. "Look how deep the hole is they've dug. If you grab for the watch now, you'll fall into the hole with that shovel-swinging maniac. No, we must wait for the right moment." He glanced at Hermann and added, "I'm only thinking of your safety."

"Thank you, Rolf," said Hermann, a bit dubiously.

"You're welcome, Hermann."

So the cats waited behind the gravestone.

It began to rain. And lightning. And thunder. That is to say, it began to get quite miserable out.

On any other night, in weather like this, the cats would have been curled up in that dry spot under the swing on the porch of the Bichon's house, or nestled in the warm straw up in the loft of the hotel stable, or asleep behind the steaming brew kettles of the Dunkelhaven brewery.

But tonight they could do nothing but wait. And watch. And get wet. And cold. And more wet.

The two men finally completed their gruesome task, uncovering the wooden casket in the bottom of the grave. They unceremoniously smashed it open, then struggled to lift the stiff, pallid corpse up out of the rain-filling hole.

The cats were aghast. "What on earth are they *doing*!?" cried Hermann, as he thought about fainting.

Rolf just shook his head, "I've seen humans put their dead *into* the ground. Never take them *out*!"

Doctor Frankenstein and his assistant dragged the body to their cart and tossed it roughly into the box, slamming down the lid. Then they climbed aboard and rode away.

The damp cats dashed from behind the gravestone and leapt unnoticed into the back of the cart. They scuttled forward and huddled together under the seat.

Hermann eyed the long box and said uneasily, "I don't like thinking about what's in there!"

"Then don't think about it." Rolf said sharply.

"How can I *not* think about it? I just saw it go in!"

The cart jounced along in the pouring rain for what seemed like a very long time. But eventually it stopped, and Doctor Frankenstein and Fritz climbed down again.

Rolf and Hermann stretched up and peered out.

"Where are we now?" asked Hermann.

"I'm sure I don't know," answered Rolf, looking around. He was unable to get his bearings because they were somewhere they'd never been before — the town gallows.

A bolt of lightning rather morbidly lit up the body of a man hanging at the end of the rope. His story is a bit more complex than we can go into here; suffice to say he was caught doing something bad, summarily hanged by the local authorities — and left hanging as an example to other would-be wrong-doers. It was rather a graphic time, 1810. His name, by the way, was Dedrick, and he had a tattoo on his right hand. It was, ironically, the silhouette of an angry cat with its back arched.

"Ach! *Another* dead human!" cried Hermann.

"Shh!" said Rolf for what he felt must be the hundredth time on this long wretched night, but was in fact only the third.

Fritz sprinted up the gallows steps and then climbed up onto the cross beam, inching his way toward where the noose was tied.

Doctor Frankenstein walked to the rear of the cart. The cats ducked under the cart seat again as he flipped open the lid of the long box. The smell of the corpse rushed over them. Hermann positively shuddered, "I'm going to go mad!"

"No, this is excellent." said Rolf.

"Excellent?!" said Hermann, his voice rising. "And in what way do you find these morbid doings excellent?"

"In this way, my dear Hermann. When the man with the watch climbs back up onto cart seat, you will leap out, hissing and spitting as you have never done before. Even though he's a felinicidal lunatic, he will not have his shovel to swing. When he is frozen in shock and surprise by your magnificent display, I shall leap up and grab the watch!"

For the first time in this long dismal night, Hermann was heartened. "Bless you, Rolf, for your way of seeing the best in the worst."

"Thank you, Hermann."

Have we mentioned that things did not go well for our two cats? Well, at that very moment, they heard the dreaded howl of Annalise! It was distant, but coming closer.

"Curse her mongrel ancestors!" hissed Rolf. "She hunts even in the rain?"

Yes, she did. Having been tipped off by a gopher who had spotted Rolf and Hermann at the cemetery, Annalise had headed there, even in the blinding rainstorm. Acker and Eckhard, slogging uncomfortably after her, doubted her sanity, but did not dare discourage her out of hope that, even if crazy, she might indeed find the diamond-eating cat. Catching the faintest whiffs of Rolf and Hermann in the stormy air, she had continued to home in on them.

Doctor Frankenstein, oblivious to the barking, grabbed the bridle of the one-eyed mule and led him toward the gallows.

Inside the cart, the cats were in a panic about the approaching hound. Rolf thought fast. "Into the box!" he ordered.

"But — but the 'it' is in the box!" shrieked Hermann.

"Into the box or die!"

"Oh well, if you put it like that!" said Hermann, now annoyed in addition to being panicked.

Doctor Frankenstein's back was to them, so the cats were able to bound into the box unseen.

They landed on top of the corpse from the grave. It was two days old, and already had a nice layer of pungent blue fungus on it — particularly pungent to cats' sensitive noses.

"I'm going to throw up!" announced Hermann.

"No, you must remain motionless and silent."

"Very well, I think I shall faint."

"I forbid it. I can't have you insensate in these fast-changing circumstances."

"Have me what?"

"You know, unconscious! Useless!"

"Rolf, *really!*" complained Hermann.

"Shh!" commanded Rolf, for the fourth time.

Doctor Frankenstein stopped the cart under the unfortunate hangee on the gallows, "Ready, Fritz!"

Up on the cross beam, Fritz leaned out and used a knife to saw at the rope.

Rolf and Hermann heard the fibrous pop of the rope's last strand giving way. And they looked up, wide-eyed as only cats can be wide-eyed, to see Dedrick's limp, rain-soaked body plummeting toward them!

They dove to either side of corpse number one just as corpse number two landed between them with a sickening, wet thump. Doctor Frankenstein stepped briskly over and slammed closed the lid of the box, never seeing the cats.

Inside it was dark, but unfortunately, as you may know, cats can see quite well in the dark, and Hermann now found himself staring into the hanged man's open bulging eyes.

"Rolf, I'm now going to stick out *all* my fur and scream!" he announced.

40

Rolf swiftly wriggled up over the second body and grabbed Hermann's head with his paws, "If you do that, we are lost. Lost! Do you hear me, Hermann? The hound is nearly upon us!"

Outside, Fritz nimbly hopped down from the gallows. He and Doctor Frankenstein boarded the cart.

But Annalise now arrived. Galloping gamely through puddles, she went round and round the cart, barking and howling. The mule bucked in his traces. Fritz fought to control him.

Annalise stretched up and put her muddy paws on the wheels as she excitedly sniffed at the box. She was delirious with success, for she could smell Rolf and Hermann plain as day, right through the overpowering dead-human odors.

Doctor Frankenstein glared at Annalise, "What is the *matter* with that animal?!"

He grabbed his cane, leaned down and gave the dog a resounding swat. Annalise yelped with pain and surprise and quickly retreated. *Why are humans so unpredictable?* she thought, *I've found the cats! They should be happy!"*

As she whined her displeasure, the two burglars caught up, puffing and dripping wet. They immediately saw that Annalise was interested in the box on the cart.

"Stop! Stop!" called Acker to Doctor Frankenstein and Fritz. He and Eckhard rushed forward and stepped in front of the mule, making it buck and kick all the more. Doctor Frankenstein jumped up and stood on the cart seat, holding his cane high.

"What are you about, blackguards?" he shouted.

Eckhard and Acker were taken aback. They had not expected to see a well-dressed rich gentleman on such a rude cart. Lowlifes like them always had to be careful about offending rich gentlemen.

Acker thought fast, or faster than Eckhard anyway, "Oh, sir, forgive us this intrusion. We were just chasing our dog."

Eckhard added boldly, "Yah, he's chased him a rabbit, he has. Chased it right into your cart. Fancy that!"

Indeed, Annalise had tentatively resumed her barking and jumping at

41

the cart, being careful to stay clear of cane-wielding Doctor Frankenstein.
"Hunting rabbits are you? At night? In a rainstorm?" asked Doctor
Frankenstein skeptically. "Nonsense! Out of our way!"

"But if we might have a look, sir, just quickly," pleaded Eckhard, "I'm
sure the critter's in there."

"Out of our way or I'll have Inspector Krogh on you!" Doctor Frankenstein threatened. The doctor, of course had his own worries. He didn't
want anyone to find out he was going around collecting dead bodies. It
wasn't something normal folk did, even in 1810.

Acker pulled Eckhard aside, then bowed to Doctor Frankenstein, "No
need for strong measures, sir! Harmless as cats we are. Sorry to have
troubled you, sir."

Acker leashed Annalise and the men stepped humbly back. Fritz
slapped the dripping reins across the mule's rump and the cart jerked
forward.

Then Acker spun to Eckhard, "*Rabbit*?!"

"Well, I didn't think he'd believe 'cats.' Why would we be chasing cats
in a rainstorm?"

"Idiot," grumbled Acker. He noticed the severed rope swaying from
the gallows. And a sobering thought struck him, "Weren't they supposed
to have done Dedrick today?"

Eckhard's eyes widened with the realization, "That's right. It *was* today.
Felt quite bad about it when I heard, us owing him money and all."

Acker nodded, then added, indicating the rope, "Odd for the hangman
to leave the rope."

"Quite odd," said Eckhard. They were well aware of proper hangman
etiquette.

They scowled suspiciously after the cart as it disappeared into the
windswept rainy darkness, and a indefinable uneasiness came over them.

For her part, Annalise was yanking wildly at her leash, nose pointed at
the cart, and barking, literally trying to be beside herself, *Why don't these
humans do something?! I found them! I found Rolf and Hermann!*

She finally got their attention. "Stupid dog is fair interested in that
cart," said Acker. "I say we follow it. See where that high-handed rich

fellow goes."

They followed. Annalise, relieved to be going in the right direction at least, thought about how to stay on the trail, for the hidden cats' scent was almost non-existent. Then she realized the scent of the mule was quite strong. All she had to do was keep track of the mule. And that's what she did.

CHAPTER FOUR

Fritz drove the cart further out of town. It jounced and bounced onward in the nasty weather. Eventually they passed Dunkelhaven's windmill, its sails spinning. Rolf and Hermann could hear its gears and shafts creaking and groaning eerily under the hiss and patter of the rain drops. As far as the cats knew, there was nothing civilized beyond the mill. Yet still the cart kept on.

Fritz turned up a twisting, forgotten, road, and at long last they came to a tall rusting gate in a high stone wall. Fritz jumped spryly down from the cart and unlocked the gate. Doctor Frankenstein drove mule and cart on through. Then Fritz locked the gate behind them.

Acker and Eckhard straggled up to the gate and looked through the bars. Having never been this far up the old road, they were as surprised as Rolf and Hermann would have been to see where they were.

The stone wall surrounded a stone watchtower. Impressive in height, nearly 100 feet, it was nonetheless very strange looking, clearly built by people of dubious aesthetic taste and engineering skill. More or less cylindrical, it appeared to grow out of a craggy stone outcrop like some sort of unfortunate black cactus. Misshapen windows pocked their way irregularly up its curved walls, offering only the vaguest hint as to the number of floors within. An unsightly patchwork of moss, mold, fungus and lichen clung to its perpetually damp flanks like skin growths. Adding to its overall unnerving impression, the tower leaned rather alarmingly to the west.

You might ask why such a thing had ever been built in the first place. Well, you see, in Europe there had been more or less non-stop warfare since pretty much the beginning of time. So there were innumerable forts, castles, fortifications, battlements, bulwarks and watchtowers scattered all over. This particular one hadn't been used for a few centuries, and thus was in extreme disrepair.

However, it was exactly the tower's uninviting nature that had drawn Doctor Frankenstein to it. He needed a workplace people wouldn't want to visit.

Unaware of the brigands spying on them from the gate, Frankenstein pulled the cart into a covered area at the tower's entrance. As he climbed down he said, "Please be so good as to deal with our new subjects, Fritz. I am exhausted and must go immediately to my bed."

"Yes, Doctor," said the obedient Fritz, "I hope you have a good night's rest."

Doctor Frankenstein unlocked the tower's imposing front door and went inside, leaving the door open. Fritz stepped to the rear of the cart. He would have to take the bodies in one at a time.

But he was in for a surprise when he opened their heavily laden box. Two cats, wet and yowling, exploded out of it and dashed off through the open watchtower door.

Startled, Fritz stood and thought about this. He remembered the frantic dog and the two lowlifes who said they were midnight rabbit hunters. Why would they say they were chasing rabbits if they were chasing cats? And why would they be chasing cats in the first place?

Fritz shrugged. He didn't know. And the doctor's work was more important anyway. He heaved the first body from the box and began dragging it feet-first toward the door.

Inside, just ahead of him, Rolf and Hermann were seeking a hiding place. The front door opened into a weird entry hall, weird because its roughly-mortared stone walls were curved in a way that made it potato-shaped. A few emaciated candles lit it to about the brightness level of a pack rat den.

The hall was no more inviting than the outside of the tower, and only slightly drier, since leaks allowed rainwater to trickle down the stones in glistening rivulets. Everywhere was the smell of mold and mildew.

The hall offered few options for hiding. It had but two exits — a heavy, iron-fitted door leading off to the left, which was closed, and, at the rear, an uneven stone staircase winding both upward and downward.

But near the stairs was a lone piece of furniture, a faded stuffed chair. Rolf and Hermann swiftly took cover under it. Knowing they were now hidden from casual human eyes, they tried to get their bearings.

Rolf sniffed disdainfully, referring to Doctor Frankenstein, "The man is obviously one of means, and *this* is his choice of domicile?"

"I quite agree, Rolf," said Hermann. "Terrible taste."

They shrunk down as Fritz entered, dragging the first body by the legs. He casually dropped it to open the side door, then pulled the body into the dark room beyond.

The oddness of this behavior was not lost on the cats. "What on earth are these humans *doing*?" exclaimed Hermann.

"None of our affair," said Rolf, trying to maintain his own composure. "Our only task is to sniff out that tall human and take his tick-tock."

And so they set out sniffing. Cats are no slouches when it comes to sniffing, by the way. They immediately noted that Doctor Frankenstein's scent lead up the stairs. And they were glad, because that meant they could avoid the room that Fritz seemed to be filling with dead bodies.

They prowled their way up the winding staircase, skipping the next two floors as the aroma trail led them assuredly to the floor second from the top. There they entered a long hallway with a number of doors.

At the far end was a bedroom, its door ajar. Inside, they spotted Dr. Frankenstein, who had just gotten into bed. He pulled up his covers, then blew out a candle on his end table.

"Perfect!" said Rolf. "He'll never see us or hear us! We'll be in, out, and gone before anyone knows it!"

"Excellent, Rolf!" said Hermann.

Staying close to the wall, they padded quickly down the hall, sure of success.

Have we mentioned that things did not go well for Rolf and Hermann this night? As they were about to pass the last room before Dr. Frankenstein's, they heard an absolutely horrible sound coming from it. It was something like snoring, but also a little like choking to death. Wet and slobbery and rattling and, well, just really horrible.

From that room, a *thing* stepped into view. And it was an inexplicably ugly thing. Twice their size, it stood on four legs, yet was not a dog, a wolf, a deer, or a pig. It had only splotches of fur. The rest was bare, wrinkled, pink-and-red-and-blue flesh. The thing's head was huge, with two ugly black holes where ears should have been. The eyes were different sizes and different *colors* — one gold and one brown. It had a tail, but that too, was ugly and naked, like some oversized rat's tail. Strangest of all, this thing had perfectly dainty, furry little cat paws.

Rolf and Hermann gaped at it, that is, with mouths wide open, which cats almost never do, because they always try to be cool. Unfortunately, the thing did not gape back. As soon as it saw them it opened *its* mouth and emitted an unspeakably chilling sound, a rasping, strangled, angry roar of pure anger.

And it charged straight at them.

Rolf and Hermann ran like there was no tomorrow, which if they hadn't have done, there wouldn't have been.

As usual Hermann trailed Rolf, hoping Rolf would think of something quick-wittedly. Rolf did. In the wall at the end of the hall, he spotted a small opening. Given the size of the thing behind them, a version of escape System Two was clearly in order.

As Rolf veered and headed for the opening, he called, "Follow me, dear Hermann! Do not falter! And leap as I do!" Though breathless Hermann said nothing, Rolf knew that he had heard and would do so.

Rolf leaped. Hermann leaped. One, two, they flew straight through the hole.

The brutish monstrosity, mere inches behind Hermann, leapt, too. But it crashed headlong into the stone, and flopped down to the floor, stunned.

Inside the hole, Rolf was pleased that his escape plan had worked perfectly. In the next second, he was less pleased to realize that inside this hole, there was no floor. Rolf and Hermann — fell.

The opening was a flue clean-out. In the past it had given chimney sweeps access to the watchtower chimney system for cleaning. Unfortunately, it also dropped about eighty feet straight down. Rolf and Hermann fell and fell, clawing wildly at the walls, barely slowing their plummet.

But landed on their feet. Because that's what cats do. However, Hermann landed on his feet rather massively on top of Rolf, who was thereby painfully flattened.

"Terribly sorry, dear Rolf!" said Hermann.

"Unavoidable, under the circumstances," groaned Rolf, with uncharacteristic understanding.

He pulled himself from beneath Hermann and they both stood still, catching their breath as best they could in a cloud of suffocating soot. They were now at the lowest chimney clean-out, in the lowest section of the tower — the basement, we might say today.

After a time, Hermann observed, "Well, I did not enjoy *that*, Rolf."

"Nor I, Hermann."

"That said, I applaud your quick-wittedness in engineering an escape from that *thing*."

"Thank you."

"And, by the way, what was that *thing?*"

"I'm sure I don't know."

"Because it quite terrified me."

"Me, as well, I admit."

Soot settling silently around them, they caught their breath a bit more. It was difficult, even for cats, to tell where they were. The small chamber's only purpose had been the removal of ash and allowing air into the chimneys above.

Hermann went on, "You saw that it had cat feet?"

"I did, but that does not aid in an explanation of what it was."

The explanation came, startlingly, from the darkness around them. A very tiny voice said, "It was the thing, Schmutz."

Rolf and Hermann both hissed, spat and arched their backs.

48

"Who are you?" blustered Rolf. Hermann was always impressed at Rolf's ability to bluster at a moment's notice. "I'll bite you, claw you, and play mercilessly with your dying body!"

"Don't! Don't!" the tiny voice shrieked in tiny fear.

"And how dare you speak to us without announcing your presence?" Rolf railed on, sensing he'd won the upper hand.

"You — you asked what the thing was," said tiny-voice-in-the-darkness.

Hermann whispered to Rolf, "It's true. We did ask."

Rolf ignored him, demanding loudly of the voice, "Well then, show yourself!"

Hermann pressed against Rolf, trembling, "Are you sure you want it to show itself? I'd just as soon not see anything else that lives in this place."

"Stay calm," whispered Rolf. "I have the upper hand."

"As you say, Rolf."

Rolf boomed, "I said show yourself!"

They waited nervously. At last, from a crack in the stone floor, five small figures inched into view — mice. A father, a mother, and three un-believably tiny babies. The babies, only days old, clung to their mother's fur.

They stared at the cats. The cats stared back.

Hermann licked his lips hungrily, "Mice!" he whispered to Rolf.

"I see that," replied Rolf.

Father Mouse crept a bit closer, gazing up at the cats as though they were from another world. "What *are* you?" he asked reverently.

Hermann's eyes went wide. If he'd been a dog, he'd have been drooling. But cats don't do that.

"They don't even know what we are!"

"I hear that," replied Rolf.

"This will be the easiest meal ever!"

"Wait," said Rolf, for he had the feeling there might be opportunity in mice that didn't recognize cats. He turned back to them. "That thing that chased us, you say you know what it is?"

"It is Schmutz, the killing thing," said Father Mouse. "The human made it."

"*Made* it?" blurted Hermann.

"Hermann, *please* don't interrupt!" hissed Rolf. Then spoke again to the mice, "The human? You mean the rich human with the tick-tock?"

Father Mouse turned to Mother Mouse with the question, "He does have a tick-tock, doesn't he?" She nodded quickly. Father Mouse turned back to Rolf, "Yes, him."

"And you really don't know what we are?" queried Rolf.

"No," said Father Mouse, still awe-inspired. "You are great, and svelte, and slinky and furry — and beautiful!"

Rolf and Hermann glanced at each other and smiled cat smiles. They couldn't agree more.

Rolf asked, "Then — you've never been outside?"

Father Mouse shook his tiny head, "We are born and raised in this great stone house. We have heard the legends of the dangers outside — of humans, of beasts called snakes, owls, and cats. So, for countless generations, our mouse-kind have lived here, safe. But then the current human came. And soon after came the killing thing, Schmutz! It is terrible, for it eats mice! Schmutz chased and chased, and caught and caught, and in time he caught and ate all the other mouse families. But not us. We are too fast, too clever. You see that we even take our young with us when we dare move about."

Rolf and Hermann knew that mouse babies normally stay in the nest until grown. "Clever, indeed," commented Rolf.

Hermann pulled him aside and whispered some more, "My dear Rolf, we have had no nourishment since the milk we stole from the kittens. You *do* appreciate how hungry I am, do you not?"

"I do, Hermann, I do. As am I. But do *you* appreciate the opportunity with which we are now presented? That is, should we choose *not* to eat these mice?"

Hermann was nonplussed, "Evidently I do not," he confessed. "I hungrily await edification."

"These mice have repeatedly escaped and outwitted that thing, Schmutz, as they call it. If we can get it to chase them, instead of us, we might much more easily gain access to the room of the human with the tick-tock. A mouse meal taken now prolongs us for mere hours. The tick-tock, once obtained, prolongs us for life."

"Well spoken, Rolf. But how do you propose that we coerce these un-schooled mice into performing the suicidal act you desire?"

"Thusly," said Rolf. And once more turned back to the patiently waiting, wide-eyed mice.

"We are gods from the world outside!" he announced.

Another quick side note, as we are striving to make a full and accurate report. Rolf did not actually use the term "gods." Animals don't practice religion as such. However, they are like humans in that they tend to come up with mythical explanations for the world's random chaos — lightning, earthquakes, forest fires and the like. Rolf made reference to animal spirit beings, and "gods" is as good a translation as any.

And so, to go on, Rolf went on, "We have come to rid your stone-house world of the thing, Schmutz, and restore to you the safety you enjoyed in generations past."

Almost inaudible mouse gasps met his pronouncement. Rolf loved it when anyone gasped at his words. He smiled as he added, "But to do this great deed, we will need you to perform a task."

"Anything!" offered Father Mouse.

"We must know a certain thing about this house, a thing you who are small and quick can tell us. You will go to the upstairs halls, go into each of the rooms off the halls, and tell us if any other humans live in them."

"Oh, we are certain there is only the tick-tock human and his helper human," said Father Mouse.

"We must be sure!" intoned Rolf with god-like authority. "There are many rooms up there. They must all be checked."

Father and Mother Mouse whispered intently to one another. Father Mouse then turned back to Rolf and spoke with a tremor in his voice, "But — the thing, Schmutz, patrols the halls."

"I did not say the task would be easy!" said Rolf. "Go now! And report back here."

Father Mouse glanced at Mother Mouse, then rose valiantly to his full height, one inch, and said, "I will do it!"

The mice disappeared back into the crack in the floor. The cats listened to their tiny paw-scratching until it faded into the distance. Then they sought a way out of the claustrophobic ash chamber. They found a wooden ladder leading to the level above, which was nothing more than a sort of intersection, with three dark, forbidding halls leading off in different directions.

Another ladder led to another level, so they chose that over the dark hallways. Up they went, entering a large room which smelled absolutely nasty — both of rotten meat and of the thing, Schmutz. A rusted, old wood burning cook stove told them the room was, or had been, a kitchen. Thankfully, a short passage led from there to the base of the watchtower's main staircase. Relieved to be now properly oriented, they headed up toward the floor with Doctor Frankenstein's bedroom.

As they went, Hermann observed, "Very strange, meeting mice who don't know what a cat is."

"But fortunate," said Rolf.

"It would have been if you had let me eat them, or at least some of them. Such an easy fresh treat. Did you see those babies, with hardly any fur?"

"Hermann, please! Don't harp on it so. I am hungry, too. But we mustn't eat them — yet. I want the thing, Schmutz to be occupied chasing that dim-witted little rodent, so that we are free to sneak into the room of the human."

Hermann thought about that for a bit, then said, "Ohhh! Then you don't even care if we find out if there are humans living in the other rooms?"

Rolf stopped and eyeballed his companion with disbelief. Sometimes Hermann's good-natured naïveté got on his nerves.

"No, Hermann. No, I don't. It's a ruse, you see?"

"Ah! That is *very* clever, my devious fellow!"

"Thank you." Rolf moved on ahead.

They reached the bedroom floor and paused in the shadows on the landing. They could faintly hear the awful gurgle-breathing of the thing, Schmutz. After a moment, they heard the infinitesimal patter of Father

Mouse's scurrying paws as he gamely carried out his mission.

Then they heard the scrabble of claws and the wet snarl of Schmutz as he spotted Father Mouse and went after him!

Rolf peeked around the corner. He caught sight of Schmutz's naked tail disappearing into one of the rooms off the hall.

"Now!" he whispered. He and Hermann scooted down the hall, silent as gliding birds, and slipped into the room at the end — Doctor Frankenstein's bedroom.

Doctor Frankenstein was in bed, asleep. Again, they paused to listen. *Tick-tock! Tick-tock!* The watch was somewhere close. There! On his nightstand! They slunk along the wall, around the room, and at last to their goal.

Rolf stood on hind-paw tiptoe and was just able to hook the watch's delicate chain with his teeth. Carefully, carefully he pulled the chain off the stand so that the watch swung down and dangled under his chin without touching the floor.

He and Hermann hurried back out.

"To the docks!" Rolf whispered triumphantly through his clenched teeth.

"To the docks!" echoed Hermann happily.

As they passed one of the other rooms, they could hear Schmutz pawing and snarling inside. Evidently he'd still not caught Father Mouse.

Distracted by the noise, they failed to notice Fritz coming up the stairs, unbuttoning his jacket, heading for his own room. They practically ran right into him!

They skidded to a stop. Again, stares were exchanged. In particular Fritz stared perplexed at the watch hanging from Rolf's mouth.

"Here now, cat" said Fritz to Rolf, stepping toward them, "Let's have that."

Rolf vigorously tried to snake past Fritz, but the young man was quick and dove on him, catching him by a hind leg. Rolf hissed and spat and scratched. Fritz recoiled and let go but, in hissing and spitting, Rolf had dropped the watch!

There was nothing they could do about it. The flummoxed cats zoomed on down the stairs. Cats are normally very cool, but when caught red-handed like that, they just get flummoxed.

Fritz stood, rubbing the bright red scratches on his hand as they began to ooze blood. Then he picked up the watch, quite mystified. Then Doctor Frankenstein burst out of his bedroom, hair disheveled and nightgown twisted unflatteringly around his bony frame.

"What is all this noise out here?" he demanded.

"Sorry, sir. There are — cats," said Fritz.

"Cats? You mean Schmutz?"

"No, sir. Other cats."

But then Doctor Frankenstein noticed what Fritz was holding, "Is that my watch?"

"Yes, sir. The cats had it."

Doctor Frankenstein blinked once, then asked dubiously, "Cats came into my bedroom and took my watch?"

"It appears that way, Doctor."

Frankenstein straightened his nightgown, then stalked down the hall and snatched the watch from Fritz. "I am very tired. And *you* are obviously very tired. To bed!" He stalked back to his bedroom, slammed his door and locked it.

"Yes, sir," said Fritz, turning to look down the stairs where the cats had disappeared. Then a sudden noise behind him made him jump. It was Schmutz, who galumphed out of one of the side rooms and snorted angrily. He had failed to catch Father Mouse.

Far below, down in the potato-shaped entry hall, Rolf and Hermann hid under the stuffed chair. "I still contend it was an excellent plan, dear Rolf," offered Hermann.

"Failure is failure," replied Rolf dismally.

"Come, come, we haven't failed, we have had a set back. We will simply await our next opportunity."

In the distance, the town church bell rang, a faint, melancholy warble limping along on damp air. Both cats winced, for, while they did not know what hours were, they knew the bell meant time was passing. From a small window high above the entrance doorway, a thin shaft of moonlight felt its way uncertainly through the musty air and glinted in Rolf's eyes. He glared up at the moon as he said, "The opportunity had better come quickly, for all too soon, instead of the town's bell, it will be the ship's bell we hear ringing."

A ghostly voice startled them both half to death, "Oh, great gods of the Outer World!" Rolf and Hermann looked up toward the sound. Father Mouse was perched in a crevice in the wall above the chair, staring down at them with his black pinhead eyes.

"I returned with my report, but you were not where I left you. I have searched high and low, literally."

"You're alive?" remarked astonished Hermann, licking his lips.

"The thing, Schmutz has never caught me yet," replied Father Mouse proudly. "I bring you the information you have asked for."

"The what?" growled Rolf, disinterested.

"The information, which is: no human other than the two you have seen lives in the other rooms off the halls."

"Ah, that, of course. Excellent," mumbled Rolf.

"We are overjoyed that you will now rid us of the thing, Schmutz! I will tell my mate!" cried the mouse ecstatically, and he disappeared back into the crevice.

Hermann sighed and said, "You should have let me eat them."

"Perhaps, perhaps," admitted Rolf. And they curled up as comfortably as possible under the chair on the cold stone floor. Hermann always laid his bushy tail across Rolf's thinner-furred back, which Rolf always appreciated.

Chapter Five

A sudden clanging woke them, echoing through the cavern-like tower. It was the bell at the courtyard gate, which callers could ring by pulling a rope. It meant, of course, that someone might soon be entering the hall. Rolf and Hermann shot from beneath the chair, leapt up the uneven stones of the wall and landed on the ledge of the high window above the entrance. Safely hidden there, they watched.

Soon, Fritz hurried down the stairs, buttoning his jacket as he went, and crossed the hall to the door, where he squinted through a peep hole. Startled at who he saw, he quickly unlocked the door and hurried out. Rolf and Hermann spun around to watch through the window, which overlooked the courtyard.

The rain had stopped. Morning sun gold-rimmed the wet cobblestones as Fritz crossed the courtyard to open the gate.

An elegant coach entered, pulled by two well-groomed horses and driven by a well-dressed coachman. He stopped, swung down, and opened the coach door. Out stepped a young woman enfolded in a fashionable, high-waisted dress of pastel pink, topped with a wide-brimmed bonnet. She tipped her head up. As the sunlight fell across her pale, clear-skinned face, resting like a pearl in a oval of golden hair, she looked rather magically out of focus. However, only one aspect of this vision impressed Rolf and Hermann: her bonnet was decorated with exotic blue bird feathers.

"Bird!" gurgled Hermann. Rolf slapped a paw over Hermann's mouth.

"Frau Elizabeth!" Fritz exclaimed to the young woman, "How is it you have come all this way?" He ushered her into the entry hall. Above, the cats spun around to keep watching.

"I must see Victor," said Elizabeth to Fritz. "I'm very worried about him." (Curiously, the most famous movie versions of this story have Doctor Frankenstein's first name wrong; Hollywood loves to change things for no reason.)

Fritz spoke quickly, defensively, "But we have been working day and night, you see —"

Doctor Frankenstein hurried down the stairs, tying the sash of a black silk robe emblazoned with the same ornate "F" as his carriage and handkerchiefs.

"Elizabeth! Great Heavens, what are you doing here?"

She rushed into his arms, "Oh, Victor! I'm so upset with you. You've been up here for weeks!"

"Please won't you go away?"

"What?!"

"I mean, won't you trust me just for a few more days?"

"Oh, you're ill! What's the matter?"

"Nothing, I'm quite all right, truly I am. Oh, can't you see I mustn't be disturbed? You'll ruin everything. My experiment is almost complete."

"I understand — and I do believe in you, Victor, but —"

He interrupted, "Of course you do! I never doubted it." (In our defense, the above confusing interchange is completely accurate. Victor and Elizabeth had a habit of speaking to one another in non sequiturs).

Doctor Frankenstein took Elizabeth's arm and led her back toward the door, "Now really, it will be just one or two days, at most, I promise. And this dank old place is no place for you. Please return to father's house. He'll be worried about you."

"Silly Victor, he knows I'm here. He condoned my coming. He's as concerned about you as I, you know."

"Then I say to both of you, just a little while longer. I'll race down to town the moment we're done, I promise. Now run along. I'm sure you have much left to plan."

"One would hope you would be part of the plans," she sulked.

"Now who's being silly? You know perfectly well I don't know the first thing about plotting such society affairs. I trust your decisions completely."

He hugged her, then kissed her hand. She sighed, but reluctantly turned to the coachman, who took her arm and led her out. Girls got led around by the arm a lot in those days.

The coach rattled away and Fritz went out to lock the courtyard gate. On the window ledge, Rolf and Hermann were bored to tears because, as noted elsewhere, they hadn't understood a word that had been said.

But now they heard a new clank and clatter. Below them, Fritz was unlocking the stout door which led off the entry hall. He strained to push it open on creaking hinges.

"Ready, Doctor!" he called, leaving the door open as he went inside.

"Yes, yes!" replied the doctor excitedly, and jogged back upstairs. In a short time he came down, now dressed for the day. As he passed below the cats to enter the room Fritz had opened, their tails snapped straight up in unison — the watch fob was dangling from his waistcoat pocket!

Even more tail-straightening, the men left the door wide open! At once the cats sprang down and sneaked into the room. They did not know it was called The Laboratory.

Once inside, Rolf and Hermann whisked silently behind a stack of oak barrels and surveyed from hiding. Cats would do absolutely everything from hiding if they could. They just love being in hiding.

The room was gigantic. Not only gigantic, but downright strange, since it was somewhat cone-shaped. The walls leaned dizzyingly inward as they rose, making it feel like the whole place was in an arrested state of caving in. Thick wooden beams crisscrossed at odd angles all the way up to the shadowy ceiling, fifty feet above them in which, glowing dimly, was a large glass skylight. There were only a few other windows, all securely barred.

One thing about the lab struck Hermann much more strongly than oddness of its shape. He wrinkled his nose woozily, "This place smells *awful!* Like — like a butcher shop!"

"I noticed," said Rolf grimly. They were quite familiar with that smell, having robbed the Dunkelhaven butcher many times. But it was unsettling to encounter the odor in this apparently-not-a-butcher-shop place.

From cat height, they could not see Fritz or Doctor Frankenstein. "Come on," Rolf said, and they crept noiselessly to the next available hiding place. But in the doctor's domain, even the hiding places were strange. The spot Rolf chose was behind a huge black enigmatic machine.

Hermann perused the back of the machine, a snake's nest of rubber-coated wires linking copper electrical contacts.

"What is this thing?"

"I'm sure I don't know," said Rolf, glancing at it, "but he certainly has a lot of them."

Indeed, there were machines of all shapes and sizes. They dominated the room, spaced around the outer walls like brooding statues in some *avant garde* church. They were like nothing the cats had ever seen before, not even in the richest houses of Dunkelhaven. Of course, they were like nothing almost *anyone* had seen in 1810. Doctor Frankenstein was, to put it mildly, very high tech. Even his pocket watch was quite the *avant garde* accessory in those days.

Still searching, the feline duo slunk forward. But from somewhere ahead, the doctor called out, "Let's have the lights, Fritz."

Hearing Fritz's footsteps coming their way, they quickly slipped behind another of the hulking machines. They shrank fearfully against the wall, for he continued straight toward them. But then he stopped and casually reached up to pull a large lever that sprouted from the front of the machine.

As Fritz walked away, the machine buzzed, an unfamiliar sound to match its unfamiliar look. Then, all around the room, electric lights glowed to life, each a hundred times brighter than any candle.

The cats would have remarked on this magical lighting, but they were far more upset by what happened to *them* at the same instant. Their skin tingled and their fur fluffed up with a life of its own, like it'd been blow-dried.

"Ahhhhch!" cried Hermann. "What is that? It feels terrible!"

"Yes, it does," agreed Rolf, trying to hide his nervousness.

Hermann then identified what the feeling felt like, "It's like — like when lightning strikes close! That human must have lightning in these big black boxes!" Hermann mashed himself even harder against the wall to get as far as possible from the humming machine.

"That's ridiculous," sniffed Rolf. "No one, not even humans, could put lightning in a box."

Of course, Rolf could not know how right Hermann was. Doctor Frankenstein's machines were powered by electricity. and it was the static discharge now making their fur stand on end.

"Oh *feathers!*" complained Hermann, looking over his shoulder and then under his legs, "I'll have to lick myself for an hour to look normal again!" ("Feathers" is a cat swear word, stemming from the disgusting feeling of feathers in one's mouth, an unavoidable side effect of bird eating.)

Hermann saw with alarm that Rolf had moved ahead, and he hurried to catch up. Rolf, searching for Doctor Frankenstein, leapt onto some sturdy shelves which held row upon row of large glass storage jars. Hermann followed. The jars, filled with murky liquid, were of a size perfect for sneaking along behind if you were a cat.

As they tip-toed from jar to jar, they could now look down on the lab. Besides the big machines, it was absolutely jammed with scientific equipment — microscopes, surgical supplies, magnifying glasses, flasks, test tubes, beakers and retorts. Indeed, every level surface was piled high. Frankenstein, while high-tech, was not the neatest of scientists.

The cats froze as Fritz walked past below them. Now he was lugging a tub filled with some sort of viscous liquid, red and gloppy. He carried it to, of all things, a roaring incinerator, flames licking out through the grate of its iron door. Fritz kicked open the door and flung the contents of the tub inside. With an angry sizzle and a blast of steam, the red stuff was devoured by the flames. Fritz slammed the grate.

"Why do they have a fire on a perfectly warm day?" asked Hermann, ever more baffled.

"I think we've already established that these are very strange humans," said Rolf dryly.

"That we have. Oh me, that we have," said Hermann, ever more nervous.

Rolf moved on. But Hermann remained rooted, for he had noticed something more upsetting than all the preceding sights. He had noticed what was in the jars. He glanced wildly from one to the next. They held parts of *formerly living things*. There were human hands and feet, arms and legs, kidneys and spleens and who-knew-what. But much, much worse, some of the jars contained animal parts. *Cat* parts! Paws and legs and bodies — and heads with ghoulish, milky staring eyes!

He scooted forward and swatted Rolf on the rump.

"Rolf! Rolf! Look!"

Intent on the search, Rolf was annoyed, saying "Now what?" as he followed Hermann's frenzied gaze. Then his whiskers twitched and his ears flattened involuntarily. And he added in a low voice, "Oh my —"

"Oh my, *indeed*!" rejoined Hermann. "Does this not exceed 'strange' by a large margin? Have we not now established that, in all our encounters with unsavory humans, we have never, *ever* encountered any this unsavory?"

"Duly established, and duly noted," Rolf concurred. "And all the more reason to complete our mission and escape this place, this town, this country, and this continent! Stop staring at the jars and come on." He led Hermann to the end of the shelves and they peered down.

Doctor Frankenstein was in the center of the room, standing at a massive table, and working on something mostly covered by a sheet. The table itself was unusual, for it was made of iron. Rolf and Hermann had snuck into enough houses to know that ordinarily you didn't make a table out of iron. Nor did you attach to it all manner of strange ornaments (insulators and electrical connections). Nor did you support it with very long chains that extended up to the distant roof, looped over pulleys, and ran all the way back down to large hand cranks mounted on the wall.

Well, to be absolutely truthful, which is our goal, Rolf and Hermann paid little attention to the table's finer details. But since these became important later, we thought we'd let you know about them now.

No, there was only one detail in the scene of interest to the cats.

Frankenstein was now wearing a grimy, stained working man's jacket. You may have seen movies or drawings in which he is depicted wearing a white lab coat, but in reality those had not yet come into fashion. As we've said, we are offering the full true account of these events. He had removed his nice clean waistcoat and draped it over a nearby chair. The lightning bolt watch fob dangled from the pocket.

"There! The tick-tock is there!" whispered Rolf. He looked around, mind working, and his eyes narrowed in a way that made him look even more Siamese. "I have a plan!"

"I trust the last step is us leaving quickly," said Hermann.

"It is." Rolf pointed his ears at one of the cross beams. It spanned the room almost directly above the chair. "I will go up onto that beam. You will get close to the human." He now aimed his ears at a pile of packing crates at the head of Frankenstein's table. "Slip behind those boxes. When I signal, you will jump out and startle the human. I shall leap from the beam and snatch the tick-tock!"

Hermann's ears drooped, "I should like to be the snatcher for once. Why must I always be the startler?"

"Because you are so very, very good at it, my dear Hermann. Now, let's do this quickly."

Hermann sighed and nodded. They split up. Hermann backtracked along the shelves, leapt down and scuttled across the lab, ducking under machines, behind piled sacks of chemicals. Soon he'd reached the packing crates. He jumped noiselessly up, hid behind the topmost crate, and waited.

Meanwhile, Rolf circled unseen behind Fritz, bounded to the top of one of the machines, nimbly tight-roped along an electrical cable, and hopped onto the cross beam. In a few cat steps he was above the chair on which Doctor Frankenstein's waistcoat hung. He scrunched down and wiggled his butt, tensing his muscles for his leap. Then nodded to Hermann below.

Hermann nodded in return and began his own butt wiggling, nervously rising up to peek over the top of the crate. But, just as he was about to make his best startle-leap, he saw what the doctor was actually working on. It wasn't good.

There was a body on the iron table — well most of a body. It had only one leg. Worse, the top of the head was missing and the skull was empty. Still worse, Doctor Frankenstein was busily sawing off its right arm! You see, Doctor Frankenstein (and quite possibly you already know this part) was assembling a made-to-order human being from spare parts he'd collected. On a nearby table were the two newest bodies — the one he and Fritz had dug up, and the one who'd been hanged, Dedrick. Today's work involved attaching a new leg taken from the dug-up body; attaching Dedrick's right arm; and also installing Dedrick's brain in the currently empty head.

As Hermann stared, the doctor removed the unwanted right arm, held it to one side and casually dropped it. Hermann was mesmerized. The arm seemed to fall in slow motion, rotating so that for an instant the fingers of its upturned hand were pointed at him in that "Here, kitty" gesture humans so often made. Then the arm landed in a large tub.

Now he gaped at the tub. *It was brimming with other discarded body parts!* At that point, poor Hermann really had no choice in the matter. He fainted.

Now, when cats faint, they go so amazingly limp that they almost flow like water. In this case, Hermann flowed off the crate and plummeted right into the tub of parts with a soft, almost inaudible — SPLAT.

Up above, Rolf was appalled, muscles spasming with his interrupted leap.

Engrossed in his operation, Doctor Frankenstein had not noticed Hermann. He called out, nodding his head at the tub, "Fritz, these are starting to smell. Please be rid of them."

"Yes, Doctor," said obedient Fritz. He hurried over and picked up the tub. But he didn't notice unconscious Hermann either, for he made it a point never to look at the contents of the tubs. After all, they were gory and revolting. He always held his breath and turned his head away when lugging a tub over to the fuming incinerator.

Seeing where Fritz was carrying his friend, Rolf was now completely agog. His plan had gone from cleverly efficient to catastrophically disastrous.

Fritz kicked open the incinerator door. Flames shot out! He raised the tub, tipping it toward the crackling blaze!

But now Rolf was sailing through the air, having leapt like never before in his life, legs spread wide like an oversized flying squirrel, though we admit he would have hated that simile. It had taken every ounce of strength, but he reached his target — the top of Fritz's head.

He came down hard, digging in his claws. Startled Fritz reeled backward. The tub flew up, flipping over and over, its contents arcing out in a lurid crimson corkscrew.

Everything glopped to the floor, with Hermann in the center of a grotesque puddle best left un-described. He came to, blinking like a bewildered baby.

Fritz slipped in the gore and fell on his butt. Rolf leapt off him and cannon-balled over to Hermann shouting, "Wake up, dear Hermann! And RUN!"

It was exactly what Hermann had wanted to do since entering this nightmare place, so he did. And the two of them shot out of the lab.

Doctor Frankenstein had turned at the sound of the tub clanging to the floor, but had not seen Rolf and Hermann's exit. All he saw was Fritz, lying in the mess. "Good God, man! Be more careful."

"It was — those cats!" protested Fritz, pointing toward the door. But there was now nothing to point at.

"Cats? Cats? You never used to be one to make up excuses! Just clean it up!" And the doctor went back to his grisly sewing project.

Before following the doctor's order, Fritz marched angrily across the lab and slammed the sturdy door, locking it.

CHAPTER SIX

Hermann obsessively licked his wet, stained, matted fur. "Disgusting! Disgusting! Disgusting!" he hissed between laps. They were again on the window ledge above the entry hall.

"Hermann, please —" began Rolf, impatiently.

But Hermann cut him off, "I do *not* please! You were not the one who fell into that tub, were you? *Were* you?"

"No," conceded Rolf, "I'm sorry, dear Hermann. You *are* disgusting."

"Thank you!" Hermann huffed, his tongue covered in fur. He spat it out and continued licking. "Who *is* this hateful human? Why does he collect dead humans and — and take them apart — and put them back together?! Does he think they shall jump up and walk about?"

"I'm sure I don't know, dear Hermann."

Rolf gazed dejectedly out the small window. It was higher than the courtyard wall, and so offered a view of the valley. He could see the windmill, and the rutted dirt road winding its way through fields already tinged with spring green. At the end of the road was Dunkelhaven, rather idyllic looking at this distance. Rolf could even see the masts of the Eagle in the harbor. This ledge would have been a very nice cat perch had things not been so grim. The church bell rang faintly. Rolf and Hermann moaned in unison. Then they were jarred by the jangling of a much closer bell, the one at the courtyard gate.

"What's this?" Rolf whispered, his ears tweaked forward.

They looked down. Eckhard, Acker and Annalise were outside the gate, Acker vigorously yanking the bell rope.

"Ach!" Hermann jittered, his mouth again full of fur, "It's that awful Annalise! She's led her awful humans here!"

"I see, I see," said Rolf glumly.

Indeed, Acker and Eckhard had been there all night. Fearful of further angering Doctor Frankenstein, they had waited until mid-morning to try ringing the bell. Acker now jangled it again.

Inside, below Rolf and Hermann, Fritz came out of the lab, being sure to shut its door behind him. Then he unlocked the tower's front door and hurried across the courtyard.

"What is it? Who are you?" he demanded through the gate's bars.

"Oh, sir!" said Acker, affecting a submissive tone, "We are but poor beggars willing to do any chore you might have, and seeking only the payment of a bit of food from your table. A mere scrap." What they really wanted, of course, was to get into the tower.

Fritz eyed them suspiciously, "I know you. You are the rabbit hunters."

"Poor beggar rabbit hunters, sir" said Eckhard quickly, "who've caught nary a rabbit in days."

"I cannot help you," said Fritz. "My master is a very busy, and very *important*, man. I dare not interrupt him for your petty wants! And anyway we have no work that needs doing. Away with you!"

Above, Rolf and Hermann nervously pressed their faces against the window, and were relieved to see Fritz walk back into the tower and slam the door. Simultaneously, Eckhard and Acker exchanged angry glances and retreated from the gate.

"He did not let them in!" exulted Hermann.

"The human with the tick-tock is rich, and they are poor," observed Rolf. While they did not understand human language, it was nevertheless easy for cats to ascertain human pecking order.

"Like us," added Hermann.

"We are not poor!" sniffed Rolf. "We are elegant and sophisticated, lacking only the means to live as we deserve."

"Of course," said Hermann quickly. "I did not mean to imply otherwise."

Outside the courtyard, Eckhard and Acker were discussing the same issue.

"Rich *schwein!*" ranted Acker. "Denying beggars even a thaler!" (A thaler was the current coin in the area.)

"No better than his stingy father, the Baron," agreed Eckhard.

"We must make a note to rob the father some time."

"Good idea."

While they complained, equally unhappy Annalise lurched back and forth in front of the gate, howling helplessly. It had taken Herculean effort just to drag her impossibly dense humans this far. Now she was doing everything she could to convince them the cats were in that watchtower!

"See how the dog strains," said Eckhard. "Surely the cats must be in there." He looked up at the sinister building and frowned, "But how are we to get in? This is not like the soft-sided houses of the rich in town. It is a fortress!"

"We wait," said Acker. "Wait and watch for our chance."

Back up at the little window, and safe for the moment from Annalise and the knife-wielding humans, Rolf and Herman's thoughts turned back to their primary problem.

"What are we to do about the tick-tock?" Hermann wailed. "The rich human's churlish assistant now keeps the door closed at all times!"

"We wait," said Rolf. "Wait and watch for our chance."

CHAPTER SEVEN

Their chance was not to come until much later. Fritz and Doctor Franken-stein remained sealed up in the laboratory for the whole day. The distant church bell rang many times, making them wince each time.

The sun was setting when at last the laboratory door opened. The cats watched eagerly from their ledge. Doctor Frankenstein stepped out, ob-viously very tired.

"We've done well, today, Fritz. Our subject is ready. As soon as the weather is right, we shall take the final step!"

"Yes, sir," said Fritz, joining him. "And we shall prove wrong all those who have spoken against your ideas."

Rolf pointed excitedly at the doctor, who was still wearing his work jacket, "Note! He does not wear the garment with the pockets. He's left the tick-tock in that big room!"

But Fritz was now glancing around suspiciously. Up on their ledge, the cats squeezed themselves against the window where he could not see them. Even so, he quickly locked the laboratory door.

"No!" lamented Hermann softly.

Doctor Frankenstein walked to the base of the curved stairway and paused. "Fritz, I should go over my notes. Would you be so kind as to bring them up?"

"Right away, sir." Fritz unlocked the door and went back inside, *leaving it open.* Rolf and Hermann's ears went forward and their pupils opened extra wide in that spooky way they do when cats are really, *really* interested in something.

"There's our chance!" whispered Rolf. They bounded down from the ledge and zipped silently into the lab. Even as they entered, right behind Fritz, he remembered the door and spun about to close it. But they had already hidden, and he did not know he was too late.

He moved on and found the stack of notes Doctor Frankenstein had asked for. Then he left the laboratory, locking the door behind him. Rolf and Hermann stepped from behind their hiding place.

"We're trapped!" said Hermann.

"Nonsense," said Rolf. "We'll find the tick-tock, then, at worst, wait by the door, all night if we have to, and fly out the moment they open it."

"Ah, of course. I so admire your ability to think ahead, dear Rolf," said Hermann, reassured.

And so they set about searching the dark and silent lab. The jumble of machinery, shelves and tables made it rather maze-like. To get oriented, Rolf sprang to the top of one of the hulking electrical machines. This particular one featured two large disks mounted side-by-side barely an inch apart. The disks were made of pie-shaped pieces of glass. Rolf paid them no mind, of course, as he squinted across the dark space.

"Over there, I think. It was near that table with the — you know, on it."

"I do know, and don't remind me," sulked Hermann.

As Rolf prepared to jump back down, he noted a handy lever sticking out of the machine about half way to the floor, and he lightly dropped onto it to make his jump easier. But as he landed on the lever, it swung down.

The machine surged to life! The two glass disks began to spin in opposite directions. As the glass plates whirled madly past electrical contacts, sparks zapped out between them like gunshots fired through the spokes of a wagon wheel. It was very loud and made Rolf and Hermann's ears hurt as they scampered away from the machine.

"What did you *do*?" demanded Hermann.

"Nothing! I jumped!" defended Rolf.

"But it's so loud!" cried Hermann, referring to the sizzling, crackling machine.

"I can't help that, can I?" said Rolf, and ever purposeful, he headed on toward the table with the dead body on it. Doctor Frankenstein's waistcoat still hung on the nearby chair. Rolf leapt onto the chair and yanked the watch from the pocket.

"You've got it!" called elated Hermann.

But just then the laboratory door flew open. There stood Fritz. From his room upstairs, he'd heard the electrical machine start and had hurried down to see what was going on. He turned on the electric lights and immediately saw Rolf and Hermann. He was astonished. Here again were those same cats, the sly-looking one again holding Doctor Frankenstein's watch!

Rolf and Hermann dashed for the open door, but Fritz stepped back and slammed it before they could get there. As the cats changed course, Fritz snatched up a length of spare copper cable and, using it like a whip, smacked it viciously against the door as a test. It left a nasty gouge of raw wood, and a malevolent look came to his eyes. It was a look Rolf and Hermann had seen in humans before. It meant, "I've got you now, cats!"

Normally, escape System Two would have been preferred, but they had the disadvantage of being trapped in the lab. The only hope was to avoid Fritz and seek some place where he could not reach them. Without really thinking it through, Hermann began with a System One maneuver, a sudden reverse, running back straight at the pursuer. This had the unexpected result of causing Fritz to trip. That led to several more unexpected results which, as you will see, set the course for the entire rest of our story.

Fritz flew headlong into another machine, hitting its levers and turning it on. This one unleashed terrifying electric arcs that crackled around and around the lab, leaping among a series of copper towers, sizzling, dancing, hissing and writhing like snakes full of fireflies. The white-hot bolts lit the lab in blinding staccato madness — a nightmare non-stop thunderstorm.

Rolf and Hermann were momentarily immobile, dazzled by the display.

Hermann shouted over the din, "I *told* you he had lightning in the machines!"

"I accede to your previous observation," Rolf admitted.

Fritz had gotten to his feet. Ignoring the crackling machine (big mistake), the furious man pursued Rolf and Hermann anew. They ran, they cornered, ducked under, leapt over. Fritz stayed close behind, swinging his deadly copper cable. With one wild swing he smashed a table full of beakers and test tubes. Glass fragments flew, flashing brilliantly in the pulsing electric light show.

Heads and ears down against the rain of glass, the cats instinctively tried a variation on System One, splitting up. Rolf went left, Hermann right. Hermann dodged between two large barrels, but realized too late they were against the wall — a dead end. He about-faced to run back out, but found Fritz directly in front of him, rearing back with the cable to strike. However, with that final fateful frenzied flail, Fritz swung his cable up *through* one of the overhead arcs of high voltage.

It was a dreadful thing to see. The energy lit Fritz up like some hell-spawned Christmas tree. He was catapulted backward into one of the tall shelves loaded with jars of pickled body parts, chemicals and who-knew-what. The shelves rocked back against the wall, then toppled forward, landing on him with a devastating crash! He was drenched in evil chemicals and preservatives. Liquid spread across the floor, shorting out cables. Electricity now leapt everywhere, shooting through the foul-smelling liquids, and through stricken Fritz.

We must take a somewhat breathless moment here to mention that, outside, Acker, Eckhard and Annalsie were staring through the bars of the courtyard gate with rapt attention. Never had any of them heard eerie sounds or seen eerie lights like those which now pulsed from the laboratory windows.

"What do you suppose that is?" whispered Eckhard. Acker could only shake his head. Annalise, while also awestruck, had a suspicion that, somehow, The Hated Rolf and Hermann were the cause. And she was right.

Back inside, Rolf and Hermann were stock still, spellbound by the sight of Fritz's predicament. But the electrified liquid splashed around Rolf's paws, giving him a mini-taste of what Fritz was experiencing.

"Wah-hoo-hoo-hooooooo!" he bellowed as he shot straight into the air, mouth wide. Mouth wide, of course, equaled watch released. It went flying across the room. The chain caught on one of the electrical cables which webbed the lab and the watch hung there, swaying, hopelessly out of cat reach.

Just then the lab door flew open again. Rolf and Hermann instantly dove for cover. Doctor Frankenstein, a deeper sleeper than Fritz, had finally been roused by the cacophony coming from the lab. He now stood aghast at the chaos before him.

With the watch unobtainable, Rolf and Hermann circled behind the crackling, zapping machines and slipped out the door right behind the doctor's legs, unseen.

Fritz still jiggled and twitched in a neon-fireworks show of electrified chemicals. The doctor rushed to the various machines, shutting them down. Silence spread over the lab. Fritz flopped forward on his face. Frankenstein tiptoed through the disgusting mish-mash of foul-smelling specimens and helped Fritz to his feet.

The doctor was shocked to see that Fritz was transformed. And not in a good way. The chemicals and electricity, working together, had changed him from a rather good-looking young man into a hunched-over, squinty-eyed caricature of his former self.

"Good Lord, man!" cried Doctor Frankenstein. Whatever were you thinking, activating my machines willy-nilly?! Look — look what it's done to you!"

"Not — me," croaked Fritz. Even his voice was different, strained and gravely, and with a weird accent that was hard to place. "Not — me. The — cats!"

The doctor shook his head in dismay, "Cats? Cats *again*? And where are these cats, Fritz? Where?"

Fritz looked around the room, weaving unsteadily. "Were — here, Doctor Fronshtein." Strangely, that was how Fritz now pronounced the doctor's name.

The cats in question were hidden just outside the laboratory door, where they had paused, realizing no one was chasing them.

Hermann looked indignantly at Fritz, "There seems to be a preponderance of humans wishing to kill us. It's like an epidemic!

"Well, in his case," said Rolf, "I must report that I recently jumped on his head, digging in my claws."

Hermann turned to Rolf in surprise, "Well, I must say that seems a rash thing to have done. And how is it that I missed this event?"

"You were unconscious. And he was about to dump you into their fire."

"Ah — I see. Well, in that case, I withdraw my implied criticism and offer in its place my profound thanks, dear Rolf."

"You are most welcome, dear Hermann."

Inside the lab, Doctor Frankenstein was now surveying the devastation. Smoke hung in the air like fog. His expensive machines were short-circuited. His precious jars of collected body parts were smashed. And worst, worst of all, he now saw that the body under the scorched sheet on his surgical table was smoldering. It, too, had been hit by the arcing electrical bolts.

He hurried over and pulled back the sheet. "No!" he gasped. "The brain is cooked! Charbroiled!"

Fritz limped over, limping because he now found he could only walk by dragging one leg. He stared at the fried brain. "I — sorry, Doctor Fronshtein."

"Sorry? Sorry?" snapped the doctor. "I was but a day away from the fruition of years of work — and you're *sorry*?!"

"Yes — I sorry," mumbled Fritz, averting his eyes.

Frankenstein examined the rest of the body. "Well, everything else is still usable." Next he hurried from machine to machine. "And these are not badly damaged. I can make repairs if I work earnestly. But the brain, the brain! The one from the grave was worm-eaten. The hanged man's was the only fresh one. There are no new brains to be had."

He paced in a caged-animal way, mind in overdrive; then suddenly whirled on Fritz, pointing a finger at him. "There are at the medical college one or two brains taken from cadavers. I know Professor Krauss there. He will have ensured they were preserved properly. To salvage all that I've worked for, you will go there tonight. You will take the finest brain you can find!"

"Take? *Steal* brain?" Fritz was finding his mind didn't work as quickly as it used to. The chemicals and electricity had affected it, too.

"Of course, steal!" barked Doctor Frankenstein. "Your bungling has left us no choice! Go now! I will work on the equipment. I expect *you* back before the dawn!"

Doctor Frankenstein immediately began unbolting the front panel of one of the machines. Fritz knew there was no point in protesting, so he resignedly limped toward the door. On the way, he noticed the doctor's watch, now mysteriously dangling from the electrical cable. He considered mentioning this, but feared angering his employer with unimportant details. But he also feared the cryptic cats might somehow reappear to steal the watch in his absence, so, without a word, he pulled it down and pocketed it.

In the entry hall, the cats saw this. "Curse our luck!" railed Rolf. "Now that would-be cat killer has the tick-tock!"

Fritz was shuffling toward the door, so they dashed to their hiding spot up on the window ledge. As they went, Hermann cajoled, "Patience, Rolf, patience. At least he's taken it down from where we couldn't reach it. We shall simply follow him to his bedroom."

"Ah," said Rolf, relieved. "Very clever of you Hermann."

"Thank you, Rolf."

But then, to their dismay, Fritz went out the front door!

"*Now* where is he going?" hissed Rolf. "Humans almost never travel in the middle of night!"

"*These* humans seem to do it a lot," observed Hermann.

Outside, Fritz laboriously hitched the mule to the cart. He was dismayed that he could not walk, talk, think, or see as well as he used to. Everything was now difficult. But he still believed in Doctor Frankenstein's work and felt he must continue. He hobbled across the courtyard and unlocked the gate.

Above, cat eyes watched, Hermann becoming alarmed, "He's leaving! We must follow — but Annalise and the knife-wielders are still outside the gate!"

That was correct. The burglars had even established a crude campsite in the brush near the wall, determined to watch for the cats until certain Biblical detention centers froze over.

Rolf was already pondering the problem, and a rather disagreeable solution presented itself. "This human house is large. It may have the small tunnels," he said. "If it does, we can use them to get out past Annalise."

"Oh, Rolf, not the small tunnels!" moaned Hermann.

You see, Rolf and Hermann were well versed in all ways in and out of human habitats. So they knew that the very fanciest places sometimes had "the small tunnels." It was their term for sewer lines. In an extreme emergency, sewers could be used for ingress or egress. But the emergency had to be *really* extreme.

"Would you not say this emergency is extreme?" queried Rolf.

"Yes, yes, but still, the tunnels. It's not the same for you, Rolf. You do not have long fur."

"Be that as it may, the tick-tock has left the premises. And for us to simply dash out through the gate under the very nose of Annalise is nigh suicidal, is it not?"

Hermann gave in, "I suppose."

"Come, I know where to start looking. I think I smelled one when we were down below."

With Hermann following dejectedly, Rolf jumped down and headed for the stairs.

Outside, Acker and Eckhard heard the mule cart approaching the gate. They jumped up and peeked out of their hiding place. But they saw it was only Fritz, in silhouette, driving the cart and, as Annalise showed no interest, they sat back down, disappointed.

As Rolf led the way down the stairs, heading for the old kitchen, he tried to raise Hermann's spirits, "Buck up, compatriot. We will traverse the tunnels ever so quickly, leap out in the fresh air, track down that annoying assistant, snatch the tick-tock and be gone from this place forever!"

"As you say, Rolf, as you say," said Hermann, trying to be bucked up.

They were nearing the kitchen door. Rolf sniffed the air, "Ah! I sense that I am right! Do you not smell the unique aroma of a small tunnel!"

"Yes," Hermann was dismayed to admit.

The watchtower did in fact have a rudimentary sewer line. Now we realize we have earlier made a point of the general lack of sanitation in Dunkelhaven but, you remember, the tower was quite old. Its oldest portion had been built by the Romans, and they were quite adept at things like fortresses, roads, aqueducts, baths, world domination — and sewers. Surprisingly, they weren't as good at fighting the really angry local tribes whom they were trying to dominate. The Germans kicked them out and, perhaps as a way of showing disdain for all things Roman, totally ignored the excellent sewer idea for about the next two thousand years.

Anyway, Rolf and Hermann strode boldly into the old kitchen — then recoiled right back out in great fear.

They had seen, nestled squarely in the center of the room, the thing, Schmutz. He had chosen the unfrequented kitchen as his bedroom, and was curled up asleep, never mind that his snoring sounded like someone drowning.

The cats considered this glitch in their plan. "I confess," said Rolf, "I am loathe to attempt to sneak past that dreadful thing."

"As am I, I assure you," replied Hermann forlornly. Then he sighed, "Do you not find, dear Rolf, that our luck in this current adventure is the worst we have ever had?"

"I do find that, dear Hermann. I do, indeed."

They lapsed into gloomy private silences. However, after suffering in that hopeless mode for but a moment, they heard the faint voice of Father Mouse.

He was calling down from the top of the kitchen door frame, "Oh great furred deities of the Outer World, I feel I must point out that the thing, Schmutz still lives. Have we, perhaps, failed you in some way?"

Hermann gaped at the little well-fed morsel. So near! He licked his lips, "No, No! You have done well!" he called. "Come closer and I will give you your reward."

As Father Mouse crept cautiously down, Hermann made ready to leap. But Rolf suddenly swished his tail preemptively in front of Hermann, who jerked back in mid-lunge, whispering angrily, "Again you would say opportunity supersedes supper?!"

"I would," Rolf whispered back. "Observe." And he called to Father Mouse, "Noble subject! My co-deity spoke hastily. It is simply that there are more tasks to perform."

Father Mouse, disheartened, said timidly, "I — I was sure you referred to only one task, Svelte One."

"Don't quibble. The others were implied," said Rolf. "And this night we require another, very important one."

"Ah, well, what would that be?" asked Father Mouse.

Rolf indicated the cook stove on the far side of the kitchen, "Are there food crumbs under that old human cooking machine?"

"Yes, but they are old and stale, and inedible even by us. The cooking machine has been unused for many mouse generations."

"Even so, we require that you find the freshest of those crumbs, take them to the place where you first met us, and wait for us there."

"Take stale crumbs? But, why?"

"I have no time for petty explanations! Go!"

Father Mouse's bulging black eyes bulged further. "But, Hirsute Master — now? The thing Schmutz sleeps in the very path I must cross!"

"Hah" snorted Rolf, "To ignore our requests is to live with the thing, Schmutz for all the rest of your days! For we cannot help you if you fail us!"

"Very well, very well!" said Father Mouse, trembling.

Rolf smiled and whispered to Hermann, "Get ready."

With grim resolve, Father Mouse scuttled down the door frame and scooted into the room. To reach the stove he had no choice but to pass sleeping Schmutz. As he did, the creature's ear-holes flexed weirdly. Its misshapen, dual-colored eyes snapped open! In a flash it was up and lunging after Father Mouse, who barely made it under the stove before Schmutz crashed into it with a resounding CLANG! He snorted and grunted wetly as he pawed under the old appliance.

Rolf was scanning the room. In the floor in the lowest corner was a rusted iron grille covering the ancient sewer line, easily big enough for a cat to get through.

"Now!" he whispered. And he led Hermann across the kitchen, right behind oblivious Schmutz, and down the drain.

Once they were far enough down the very smelly tunnel, Hermann commented peevishly, "I envy the thing, Schmutz his meal."

"Better he make it of that gullible mouse than of you, dear Hermann." Hermann thought about that, and shuddered. "That's true, Rolf."

Onward they went. It wasn't a fun journey, for the old sewer had what people who know about old sewers call "bellies." Those are low spots where things don't drain completely; where things collect. And none of the things that collect are pleasant to begin with. And once they collect they just get more rotten and smelly.

"I've not even finished licking off the smell from that nauseating tub," groaned Hermann. "I'll be weeks licking off this new smell!"

"Stop complaining!" said Rolf, but he gritted his teeth as he crawled along. No cat likes getting dirty, let alone filthy.

At long last, the duo flopped out of the drippy end of the sewer pipe above a sluggish stream. They crawled to dry ground and lay panting in the moonlight, evil-smelling steam rising off their slime-coated fur.

"I should like to propose," wheezed Hermann, "that, in the future, we never speak of this night."

"Agreed, agreed," nodded Rolf.

They climbed up to the Dunkelhaven road, then ran and ran. Their spirits were lifted when they finally saw the mule cart ahead of them.

Rolf said, "You must admit at least one part of the plan has gone well. By using the tunnel we have thoroughly avoided Annalise and her humans."

"That we have!" said Hermann.

This, unfortunately, was not strictly correct. Even out in the boonies, the cats could not catch a break. As they jaunted jauntily down the road, they were spotted by a vole who, being nocturnal, was tidying up the entrance to his burrow. This particular vole had never been duped, robbed, chased or played with by Rolf and Hermann, but by now almost every animal in the area had heard of Annalise's Great Hunt. So, acting on general principals, the vole passed the word along and before you knew it, an enormous eagle owl was soaring toward the watchtower.

Acker and Eckhard had already fallen asleep. Annalise was dozing fitfully when the owl passed overhead on whisper-silent wings and hooted, "Alooort! Alooorrt! The Hoooted Coooots hooove booonn spoootted!" Yes, owls sound a bit like pigeons.

Annalise let out an heart-stopping howl, and was immediately disappointed when Acker, jolted awake, smacked her across the snout, "Idiot hound!"

Eckhard then smacked Acker across the nose, "Idiot *schwein*! She's sensed something!" He untied Annalise's leash and she instantly bounded down the road for town with her hopeful masters racing to keep up.

CHAPTER EIGHT

Rolf and Hermann followed Fritz to his clandestine destination, the medical college. It was an expansive, two story stone building situated on well-kept grounds surrounded by a stone wall.

They watched as Fritz furtively pulled the mule to a stop in the shadow of some blossoming elms whose branches overhung the wall. To their surprise, he then climbed onto the cart, stood on tip-toe, and struggled over the wall.

They sprang onto the wall and continued spying. Fritz moved silently to the rear of the college. Compounding their surprise, he then snatched up a rock, broke a window, clambered through it and disappeared inside. Breaking windows was not something most humans did.

"Whatever is he *doing?*" asked Hermann.

Rolf just shook his head, baffled, "We must not let it concern us. Our only thought must be for the tick-tock in his pocket."

"But how will we get it? He does not let the chain dangle out as the other human does," complained Hermann.

"Nevertheless! We will follow him until we see opportunity!" commanded Rolf. And when Rolf said things in his commanding tone, Hermann always felt he had to obey. They hopped down from the wall, scampered across the damp spring grass, and sprang silently through the broken window.

Fritz limped down dark hallways. Stone arches rose majestically above him. His footsteps echoed softly on polished marble floors. He made each turn confidently, for in fact he knew these halls well. As this story was told and re-told in later years, it would be forgotten that Fritz had met Doctor Frankenstein here. Fritz had been a student, full of questions, ambition and impatience. He had found the doctor's volatile nature and unconventional thinking quite attractive when compared to that of his stodgy, learn-by-rote professors. So he had left school without graduating to serve as Frankenstein's assistant.

Never far behind him, two silent shadowy shapes matched his every turn. Finally, he reached his goal, the Anatomy Laboratory — a nice learned name for the place where medical students cut up cadavers. It looked quite different tonight, with moonlight pouring through its tall windows, painting everything in grey-white opalescence.

The room was spacious, the center devoted to its three dissection tables. The walls were lined with shelves filled with glass specimen jars like those in Doctor Frankenstein's laboratory, only there were many, many more of them. The moonlight made them glimmer like a thousand pale stars.

Fritz tiptoed along the shelves, searching. Rolf and Hermann, always preferring to be high rather than low, hopped onto the shelves, moving catlike, if you will, keeping pace with him.

As they skulked along, Hermann paused behind a particularly large jar, and got an upsetting feeling of déjà vu, for he saw, floating inside it, dead eyes staring out at him, belonging to the severed head of a pig.

Hermann hiss-whispered, "Rolf! Rolf, look! This place is just like that *other* awful human's place!"

Rolf slid up beside him, "I see, I see, Hermann," he said uneasily. "Still another reason to leave this awful town."

"Yes, Rolf, oh yes!" said Hermann. They scurried away from the jar and across some open shelf space to hide behind two other jars. These were in shadow and they couldn't see what was inside, which was fine with them.

Just as they were calming down, orange light suddenly lit the room. They flinched and made themselves as small as possible behind the jars.

Fritz had struck a match, as he'd been unable to find what he was look-ing for by moonlight alone. He turned slowly, squinting up at the rows of jars. Smoke from the match curled around his head and the flame glinted in his eyes, giving him a gargoyle-ish look.

He stopped, staring right at Rolf and Hermann! Actually, he wasn't staring right at Rolf and Hermann. He was staring at the jars behind which they were hiding.

Nevertheless, Hermann was panicked, "He sees us!"

"No, he doesn't have that definite 'he sees us' look," said Rolf firmly, though he was not positive.

Fritz blew out his match, grabbed a short ladder, and headed toward them.

There was open shelf space on either side of the two jars. The cats could not move left or right without surely being seen. So they stayed put.

Fritz set his ladder at the base of the shelf and began climbing.

"He's coming! He sees us, I tell you!" whispered Hermann.

"Perhaps, perhaps. If so, wait till the last second to leap. That's always the best way," cautioned Rolf.

They waited. Fritz paused to strike another match and hold it up to the jars above him, which were barely within his reach. The flame's flickering glow played through the murky fluid in the jars, lighting the cats in rippling waves.

Fritz was simply doing what he'd been sent to do. He'd found the two jars in the college collection that held human brains. He had struck the second match to read the labels, so that he'd be sure to take the best one.

His ladder was shorter than he'd have liked, so he stepped onto the very top which, as you know, you're not supposed to do. Balancing unsteadily, he grabbed the desired jar.

It was the one in front of Hermann. The instant Fritz moved it, Hermann shot out from behind it, hissing and spitting like crazy. He flew right past startled Fritz's head as he sailed out into the room.

Fritz teetered, then toppled. He and the jar hit the marble floor at about the same time, he with a muted THUD, the jar with a spectacular SMASH. The preservative liquid in the jar was pure alcohol, and its nose-burning fumes quickly spread everywhere.

Rolf, ever focused, looked down at fallen Fritz. He saw the silver glint of Doctor Frankenstein's watch fob dangling from Fritz's jacket pocket. Rolf leapt down and bee-lined for Fritz, knowing he could snatch the watch before the man could even react. But just then, as was so often the case in this rather complex adventure, the unexpected happened.

Annalise came flying into the room howling like, well, a bloodhound. Having been told where to pick up the cats' trail, it had been easy to follow it straight to the college.

Skidding uncontrollably across the polished floor, she collided with Rolf, who had been within inches of snagging the watch. They slid onward together and slammed into the shelves.

In the next instant, both Rolf and Hermann were frantically ducking and dodging Annalise's flashing teeth. But in the next instant right after that instant, Fritz managed to right himself, and he lashed out wildly at the nearest living thing, angrily kicking poor Annalise squarely in the sensitive backside. This gave Rolf and Hermann a precious split second to bolt across the room and into the hall. Annalise yelped in pain, but with hound-like dedication, galloped after the cats, her claws clackity-clacking as she tried to get traction.

Fritz stood up shakily and tried to collect himself. He could not imagine why or how the cats had appeared here to attack him yet again, or where the dog had come from. But they had all gone now, and any hope for explanation with them. Besides, he had a much more pressing problem. He struck a match and stared in dismay at the shredded brain lying among the glass shards of the jar. Next he looked up at the other jar on the shelf, holding the only other brain currently available. That one was labeled "Abnormal." Ironically, the college professors had planned to add Dedrick's brain to their collection, but of course his body had disappeared from the gallows.

In the halls, Rolf and Hermann were in a true life-and-death chase. Rolf led them unerringly back the way they had come, but Annalise pursued with lethal intensity. System One was tested to its limit. At last they saw the broken window ahead and, with a transcendental burst of speed, sailed through it.

This they did just in time to slam directly into Acker and Eckhard. The burglars, following Annalise, had only now made it to the college grounds and had been hesitantly approaching the broken window.

Hermann ricocheted off Acker's head, Rolf off Eckhard's. On landing, claws dug firmly into earth and the cats launched themselves onward over the wall. They were gone before Acker and Eckhard could so much as draw a knife, which was pretty much their first impulse when anything unexpected happened.

The burglars gawked dumbly after the felines, slowly realizing that fortune had again just eluded them.

"Th-that — was the cats!" noted Acker.

"Told you the dog knew!" Eckhard snorted.

The dizzying pace of action continued. Annalise rocketed out of the window, slamming into Acker and knocking him into Eckhard. As the men tumbled to the ground, Annalise rolled to her feet and charged after the cats.

Even as the burglars scrambled up to give chase, a light came from the window. Afraid it might be the lantern of a night watchman, they dove into the bushes and cowered.

But the lantern was held by Fritz. He leaned out and lowered it to the ground. Then he carefully climbed out of the window, carrying the second brain-in-a-jar. Worried that he might drop it, he'd risked lighting a lantern to make his way back out of the building.

Tucking the sloshing jar under one arm, he picked up the lantern, walked right past hidden Acker and Eckhard, climbed over the wall, loaded the jar carefully into his cart, and rode off.

While Acker and Eckhard were now free to pursue Annalise and the cats, they were given pause, because they'd just gotten a good look at Fritz.

"Was that Doctor Frankenstein's man?" asked Eckhard.

"Well, he — he was dressed the same," answered Acker uncertainly.

"But he looked so — *different*," pressed Eckhard.

"Yes, he did."

"But he was stealing something, wasn't he? I mean, what was in that jar?"

"It looked like a brain."

"A what?"

"A brain. You know, the thing inside your head. That's what was in the jar."

"The huge prune thing in that jar is like what's inside my *head*? You're making me sick!" Eckhard complained.

Acker ignored his accomplice's distress, "Stop it! After our hound!"

Indeed, the sound of Annalise's howls were fast fading. The two burglars wearily took off after her.

CHAPTER NINE

So here's what happened on the rest of that night:

Exhausted Rolf and Hermann kept ahead of Annalise and made it back to the sewer pipe. It was too small for her to follow them, so they were free to crawl all the disgusting way back inside the watchtower. But as they were about to climb out into the kitchen, they heard the strangled breathing of the thing, Schmutz. Having finished his nightly kill-any-thing-that-moves rounds, he was just settling down to sleep on the cold floor. The cats could not hope to steal past him, so they simply huddled together in the mouth of the sewer drain.

Exhausted Eckhard and Acker ran all the way back to the watchtower to find frustrated (and exhausted) Annalise barking and howling at the gate. But they had to drag her into hiding because exhausted Fritz then came along in the cart.

He entered the courtyard, locked the gate behind him, turned the exhausted mule into the stable, and carried the newly acquired brain into the lab.

To Fritz's relief, the lab was deserted. Dr. Frankenstein had repaired the machines and gone to bed. Fritz found a razor blade and used it to carefully remove from the jar the label which inconveniently proclaimed "Abnormal." Placing the jar on the iron table, he then returned the pocket watch to Doctor Frankenstein's waistcoat, which was still hanging on the nearby chair. Finally, he searched every nook and cranny of the lab, looking for the vexing cats. Certain they were not there, he left, locking the laboratory door.

He started up the stairs, but then realized that, over this long and chaotic day, he'd forgotten to feed the thing, Schmutz. Goodhearted fellow that he was, he turned about and headed downstairs.

In the kitchen, Schmutz cowered at the sound of Fritz's approaching footsteps. In the sewer quite near him Rolf and Hermann cowered at the sound of Schmutz.

Fritz entered, went to a large barrel in the corner, lifted the heavy lid, pulled out a maggoty piece of meat, and tossed it toward Schmutz. It slid right to the edge of the sewer drain. Schmutz pounced on it, hungrily snatching it in his snaggle-toothed jaws. A long string of his drool stretched down through the grate and onto Hermann's head. Rolf clapped his paws over Hermann's mouth to keep him from hissing and spitting in sheer disgust.

But they were still safe. Their dainty cat smell was overpowered by the odor from the sewer. Unaware of them, Schmutz scrabbled into a corner to concentrate on his lump of rancid food and make loathsome gobbling sounds.

Rolf removed his paws. Hermann brusquely combed his whiskers back into proper alignment as he said crossly, "You have taken, of late, to repeatedly clapping your paws over my mouth."

"Were you not about to hiss and spit?"

"What if I was? It's not as though the situation didn't warrant it."

"Calm, dear Hermann, calm. We must not reveal ourselves," cautioned Rolf.

"All well for you to suggest calm, Rolf. Did you not hear?"

"Hear what?" asked Rolf.

"The *lack* of ticking coming from the formerly normal human?"

Rolf involuntarily gulped as he realized what he indeed had not noticed, "He no longer has the tick-tock!"

Hermann nodded glumly, "And he has no doubt returned it to the room of lightning. You know, the room with the always-closed door."

Rolf's head drooped. "A sobering turn of events, dear friend. Yet we can do nothing about it until the thing, Schmutz, leaves."

They sank down in the fetid smelliness of the sewer pipe to wait. Eventually, they fell asleep. In fact, nearly everyone fell asleep. Everyone, that is, but Acker and Eckhard. They were too frustrated at having just missed catching the cat with the fabulous diamond inside it. So they sat in the clammy morning mist and discussed it.

"We must think the situation through," said Acker.

"Well," offered Eckhard, "We know for sure the cats was in the watchtower — and we know by the energy of our dog they have gone back there. That's sort of a silver lining, if you look for it."

"Hmph," hmphed Acker, "The cursed cats escaped our good-for-nothing dog. And Frankenstein and his lopsided helper are again sealed up in the tower. No doubt they will still refuse to let us in. And we will never reach those miserable cats!"

"You're not looking for the silver."

"Stop it! We can't simply count our blessings. Time is short! We must act! We must use our brains!"

"Please don't say 'brains.' Then all I can think about is that ugly, wrinkled —"

"All right, all right. But we must be clever. We must be more clever than we have ever been." Acker paced up and down, staring up at the watchtower. "What is that Doctor Frankenstein up to, anyway?"

"Well I don't know, Acker. And I'll claim no one in the whole town knows, or they'd be up in arms about it — him and his helper, skulking in the dark of night, carting b-b-brains about."

Acker stopped pacing, his face alight with a new thought, "You are right, Eckhard. The townsfolk *would* be fair upset to know what's afoot in this foul old place."

"Yes, I just said they would. But that doesn't help us."

"But it *might* help us. Suppose we go to town and tell the townsfolk what he's doing. Make sure they are outraged. Suggest they rise up, storm his watchtower and demand he come out and explain himself?"

Eckhard was falling behind in the logic, "And — if they did that?"

"*When* they do that, you and me is free to sneak in unnoticed and find the cursed cats!"

Eckhard brightened a bit, "Ohhh, it's a sort of plan!"

Acker paused to give Eckhard a look of disbelief rather like Rolf sometimes gave Hermann. Then they set off for town, dragging reluctant Annalise with them.

Because they were dragging her away from the building which hid the cats, Annalise was convinced they'd gone quite mad. It was one of those times when she really, really wished she could speak human. All dogs felt like that of course. They worked so hard to please their masters, yet it was so difficult to communicate even the simplest things. The world was a rich, ever-changing universe of sights, sounds and, most importantly, smells that revealed so much! Dogs wanted to say things like, "Stop dragging me! This tree has been visited by nine other dogs today alone!" Or, "There are four partridges in the bush right behind you! Can't you smell them!" Annalise sighed as she was dragged along. Such joy was never to be. She would always be reduced to straining at her leash, barking the pathetic simple terms humans understood. "Come here! Come here! Let's go! Let's go! 'Ata boy, human! Come on! You can do it! 'Ata boy!"

CHAPTER TEN

In the morning, Schmutz eventually roused himself and lumbered out of the kitchen to patrol the watchtower. Rolf and Hermann crawled out of the sewer grate. Even though they were stiff and sore and smelly, Rolf was energized with renewed purpose.

"We must spy constantly on the door to the lightning room, looking for any opportunity to enter and snatch the tick-tock."

"And what of the thing, Schmutz?" asked less-energized Hermann.

Rolf said, "We must attract the mice. If they still live, we can get them to distract the thing again."

Hermann nodded listlessly. They began to make soft scratching and purring noises that they hoped would attract mice and not Schmutz. Eventually the whole mouse family appeared under the old cook stove, having entered the kitchen via a ridiculously small hole, as only mice can do.

Had Rolf and Hermann been paying attention to anything other than their own troubles, they would have noticed that Mother Mouse was angry. But they weren't, so they didn't.

Hermann stared at the three Mouse Children clinging to Mother Mouse. Their succulent, pink skin still shone enticingly through their dainty fur.

"Look at them!" he whispered. "They're like little *hors d'oeuvres*! Can't I have just one?"

"If you eat one, what do you think the rest of the mice will do?" Rolf whispered.

"Run away?"

"And never help us again."

"But I'm so *hungry!*"

"No more so than I. Now, quiet!"

Rolf strode out to face the mouse family, trying to look grand. They shrank back under the stove, for, to them, he did. But that didn't stop Mother Mouse from poking Father Mouse in the butt with her nose. He winced uncomfortably, reluctant to speak. But then he said softly, "Oh furry Supreme Beings of the Outer World, I performed my previous task. I took the crumbs to the dark place and waited for you. But you never came."

"We were — busy. But we knew, through our general omniscience, that you had completed the task. Well done."

Father Mouse rushed on, "And yet the thing, Schmutz *still* pursues us!"

Due to all the other stress, Rolf had forgotten his promise to rid them of Schmutz. So he countered, "Ah, but have you not noticed how the beast has grown weaker?"

"Weaker!?" shrieked Mother Mouse (and a mouse shriek is very high pitched and painful). Then she poked Father Mouse in the butt again, prompting him to elaborate.

"Oh Shaggy Divine One, I do not wish to seem disrespectful, but once I left the kitchen with the crumbs, the monster chased me *relentlessly!* Twice I was cornered and had to flee under his very jaws! Once he actually struck me with his great ugly paw!"

It was not the answer Rolf wanted, but he was nothing if not adaptive, and he attempted to turn the negative into a positive, "And he most certainly *would* have caught you had we not weakened him with our fantastic powers! We intervened, and you escaped!"

Mother Mouse snorted her disbelief. But Father Mouse smacked her across the snout with his tail. She backed up submissively, but no less angry, even as Father Mouse proclaimed, "Yes! He was all but upon me, yet even so I evaded him! I see now! Thank you, O' great and glorious fur-clad Wonders!"

Having reclaimed deity status, at least with Father Mouse, Rolf quickly pressed his advantage, "You must now run to the tallest part of this stone house, making as much noise as you can. Look out from there at the town of the humans and tell us if the ship still lies in the harbor."

"A-a-all the way to the top?" stammered Father Mouse.

"All the way," insisted Rolf. "We must have this information to complete our noble task."

"But the thing, Schmutz —"

"Will not catch you, for we will make you swift and him slow — with our powers, aforementioned."

Father Mouse once again rose to his full height, "I will do it!" He and his mouse family disappeared into the darkness under the stove.

When they were gone, Hermann grumbled, "If that unnatural monster Schmutz gets to eat the mice, and I get none, I shall be quite put out with you, Rolf."

"Be happy the monster isn't eating *you*, my dear Hermann."

"You made that point earlier," said Hermann dryly.

"It is no less true now than then."

Hermann was trying to come up with a retort, but instead flinched and flattened his ears at the sound of a throaty growl somewhere far above, followed by the scrabbling of twisted claws and the racing of tiny paws. It was the thing, Schmutz, chasing Father Mouse, and that meant it was safe for the cats to leave the kitchen.

They dashed up the stairs, into the entry hall and up to their window perch. They had not long to wait. Happily, Doctor Frankenstein and Fritz came down early, the doctor very excited as Fritz unlocked the lab. Rolf and Hermann tensed, tails twitching, ready to spring and follow. Unhappily, Fritz was extremely watchful as he held the door for Frankenstein, then followed and closed it behind him. He was making absolutely certain that nothing except he and the doctor went in or out.

Rolf and Hermann sank down on their ledge. And waited. For hours. But Fritz was just as careful later in the day, when he and his employer came out for lunch. It seemed the cats would never get into the lab through that door. Furthermore, as though to complement their dour mood, great rain clouds rolled in. Lightning and thunder shook the hills. A monster storm was brewing.

CHAPTER ELEVEN

Down in Dunkelhaven, Acker and Eckhard had been plotting how best to spread the news about the goings-on up at the watchtower. As a starting point, they had chosen a *bierwirtschaft*, reasoning that people who are drinking are more easily stirred to action, or at least more easily provoked to violence. They had chosen a rather upscale *bierwirtschaft* on the theory that upscale people are more effective at getting things done. The saloon was one they had never been in, since they themselves were downscale. Ironically, it was the very one from which Rolf and Hermann had followed Doctor Frankenstein at the beginning of this increasingly ironic series of events.

The interior of the *bierwirtschaft* was appropriately woody, smoky, and dark. Its undulating, plastered walls had a mushroom-like patina. The chairs, tables and sofas spanned generations. The barman had just tapped a new keg of the local brewery's maibock, and a large number of patrons were savoring that spring beer while they smoked long, curved pipes and enjoyed soft-spoken, upscale conversation.

The burglars didn't make the best of impressions as they tied up their ungroomed hound out front and barged in with their odorous clothes, muddy boots and ratty hair. But they were the sort who didn't realize what impression they made, so they forged right ahead.

They selected as their target a young, sandy-haired gentleman dressed in a fine grey suit of the tight-fitting style just becoming popular. Leaning against the bar with studied casualness, he sipped his maibock from an elegant stoneware beer stein with an equally fancy pewter lid. German law required that all beer steins have lids, because even an upscale place like this was lousy with flies — remember those streets full of garbage? Screen doors didn't exist yet, and you hated to have flies dive-bombing your beer.

Anyway, Acker and Eckhard sidled up to the young gentleman and Acker said, loudly enough for everyone else to hear, "So, what think you of the dark doings up at the old watchtower?"

All the conversations stopped and the place went silent. The young man looked Acker and Eckhard up and down disapprovingly, "Are you addressing me?"

"We are, sir! What think you?" chimed in Eckhard, trying to imitate Acker's bold attitude.

The young man thumbed open his stein's lid and sipped his beer dismissively, "Well, it is well known that Baron Frankenstein purchased the tower for the use of his son, the doctor."

Acker and Eckhard didn't know that, but tried not to be thrown by the news. "Aye, aye, of course he did, sir!" said Acker, "But the point we're asking about is, do you know they've been seen, young Frankenstein and his manservant, I mean, prowling about the town with all manner of mysterious boxes on carts, taking who-knows-what up to that tower! And the capper, the capper, my friends, was the sight of his man making off with a brain from the college! A *human* brain!"

This assertion did get a rise from the *bierwirtschaft* patrons, but they were doubtful of any claim made by these two ill-dressed ruffians.

"A brain, you say?" asked the young man.

"Aye! What's inside your head, sir! It's — it's nasty! It's an outrage! It's — it's —"

"Sacrilege?" offered the young man.

"Exactly!" said Acker, thankful for the plum word. "That's what it is. We tell you, there's *eeevil* afoot there!"

"It is also well known," the young man said calmly, "that the younger Frankenstein pursues studies frowned upon by some professors of the college. But I doubt that even they would classify it as evil."

Acker desperately tried to bolster his position. "But there's more, sir! At night, at night you hears all manner of strange noises coming from that watchtower, and you sees lights of a color no lantern ever threw. He's doing things that — that people oughtn't to — that a person shouldn't be — that would scare even a —"

The young man again filled in for Acker's stuttering, "You suggest perhaps that he is meddling with forces not meant for mortal man?"

Acker's eyebrows went up, "You have a grand way with words, you do, sir! Yes! Suggesting that most strongly we are, me and Eckhard. And we think something ought to be done!"

The patrons glanced at each other uncomfortably. The young man, finding himself the bar's de facto spokesperson, then asked, "And what is it you would have done, exactly?"

Acker and Eckhard were flustered by the question. They'd hoped the townsfolk would be a bit more proactive.

"Well — well," said Eckhard "we think we should all march up there, as a group, you know, and demand he open his doors to us good citizens, to show he's got nothing to hide!"

Acker quickly added, "And bear weapons — you know, pitchforks and the like — and torches! So he sees we mean to enforce our wishes!"

The patrons glanced about again. The young gentleman leaned back against the bar and opened his stein. This time he sipped derisively, for he was well-educated and could perform a derisive sip better than most. "You actually think that we're going to gather into some sort of horde, take up torches and farm implements, and storm the old watchtower?"

"Well — yes," said Acker, a bit deflated. "Something like that."

The young man took another, even more derisive sip, "I mean, it's not 1650 is it? It's 1810."

Chuckles rippled around the establishment. Then a portly man with a red face and matching neck scarf spoke up, "Indeed it is, and Doctor Frankenstein is quite respected. *And* he's a doctor."

The barman leaned forward, disturbed at having one of his better customers maligned, "Not to mention his *father*, the Baron, is respected as well, and rich, and owns land all about town, *and* frequents this very *bierwirtschaft.*"

"Very true," said the young man. He turned to the barman, "I should think at most we should mention the accusation regarding the manservant to Inspector Krogh."

"At most," nodded the barman.

And that's what they did. But not until later that day, when one of them happened to run into the Inspector.

So Eckhard and Acker had to wait to see if Inspector Krogh would decide to go up to the watchtower. They lurked near his office, and lurked in alleys following him, all the while trying not to look like lurkers.

But as it happened, the Inspector was quite busy attempting to solve the mystery of who had broken into a certain house and stolen a certain very valuable diamond ring, so he didn't feel a strong desire to go all the way up to the watchtower and bother the son of richest man in town with embarrassing questions.

Frustrated Acker and Eckhard waited. And lurked. And frustrated Annalise waited. And whined. She could not understand this insane detour back to Dunkelhaven. She *knew* where the cats were, had announced it repeatedly, and yet her dimwitted owners would do nothing about it.

However, Fate, which, you have no doubt noted, had a lot to do with this story, now tossed the forlorn trio a bone. Inspector Krogh was approached by a professor from the college who informed him that someone had indeed stolen a brain. Therefore, even though normally he would never have gone out so late in the day, and especially with the weather turning sour, the Inspector decided he'd best slog it on up to the watchtower and at least make an inquiry.

Lurking as they were nearby, Acker and Eckhard overheard his decision. They were elated. Their plan was working! More or less. They raced to the edge of town and hid under a bridge on the road to the watchtower. From there they knew it would be easy to follow the Inspector undetected.

Evening descended. The storm arrived in earnest, building to furious intensity, with relentless lightning and thunder — let's admit it, Dunkelhaven was rather a dreary place. But the dedicated Inspector soon came riding along on his less dedicated and very unhappy horse, who had been looking forward to a comfortable and dry evening in the stable.

As they crossed the bridge, the horse was of course aware of Annalise and she of the horse, for animals are aware of many more things than we are. It was easy for them to have a brief conversation, which went like this:

"What are you doing out in this weather, dog?" asked the horse.

"My insane masters are following your master."

"My master is the more insane! We could get killed in all this lightning, and now he takes the road to the old watchtower-hr-hr-hr!" When annoyed, horses often add extra syllables to words ending in "r".

"My masters have been trying to get in there for two days. I think they hope your master will open the door for them."

"Why?" The horse was now some distance up the road, but he and Annalise could hear each other perfectly well.

"The cats, Rolf and Hermann, are there. My masters want to kill them."

"Oh-h-h-h!" whinnied the horse. "That changes everything. This could be fun!" And, to the Inspector's surprise, he quickened his pace.

Chapter Twelve

Up at the watchtower, spirits were unexpectedly high, not despite the awful weather, but because of it. The ferocity of the thunderstorm fit perfectly into Doctor Frankenstein's plans. After months of work, all was ready. He had installed the new brain Fritz had stolen. His sewn-together human body was again complete — waiting.

But Frankenstein had always known that, in addition to his electrical machines, what he needed to complete his grand experiment was a burst of electricity that only a lightning strike could provide. He had attached a number of copper poles to the top of the tower to help ensure that lightning would indeed strike in any major storm. This storm was major — so tonight was the night!

All this would have been very exciting if you had been in the laboratory; however, on their window ledge outside the locked door, Rolf and Hermann were, once again, bored to tears. In fact, for them, the only interesting thing that had happened for hours happened now. There was a very loud ringing of the gate bell. Loud because it had to overcome the splash, clash and rumble of the storm.

In the lab, Doctor Frankenstein was immediately angry at the interruption, "What? What? Callers at this hour? In this weather? At this time?! Send them away, Fritz! Away!"

Fritz hurried out.

Rolf and Hermann tensed eagerly as Fritz came out of the laboratory, then sagged disappointedly as he locked the door. As he turned to hobble, hunched over, to the front door, they were startled to see that his beard had grown unnaturally fast since only last night — another side-effect of his electrocution and chemical bath.

"He didn't have a beard yesterday, did he?" asked Hermann.

"Of course not," said Rolf.

"Well, that is odd, and I say again that I don't like this distasteful place or these creepy humans."

"You are on record, dear Hermann."

Fritz looked through the door's peep hole, then quickly threw the door wide and raced out into the tempest to open the courtyard gate. In a moment he returned with the Inspector. As they both shook water from their garments, Fritz called worriedly to the closed laboratory door, "Doctor Fronshtein! Inspector Krogh eez come see you!"

Rolf and Hermann tensed again as Doctor Frankenstein hurried out of the lab. But he, too, locked the door behind him, worried not about cats, but rather about this unexpected visitor. He straightened his grimy work jacket and, trying to seem nonchalant, walked over to greet the interrupter.

"Great Heavens, Inspector," what could possibly motivate a ride to my humble workshop in such weather?"

The Inspector said uncomfortably, "Sorry to trouble you, sir. Certainly I would not travel here on a triviality." He took a breath to delay briefly the next unpleasant statement, "But I have had a rather serious report that implicates your assistant Fritz in the theft of a certain — brain."

Doctor Frankenstein stiffened, trying to hide his alarm, "Er, brain?"

"Yes, from the college. I know for certain the brain is missing; and I have other, uh, less reliable evidence your assistant may have been involved."

Doctor Frankenstein glared at Fritz. Fritz shrugged helplessly.

But the Inspector went on, "So, is he here? Fritz, I mean?"

Doctor Frankenstein was taken aback. Then he realized Fritz was so changed that Inspector Krogh did not even recognize him.

"No, he is not," lied the doctor quickly. "Unfortunately, I had to release him from my employ. Quite disappointing, really. You see, I caught him — stealing."

"Doctor!" protested Fritz.

"Quiet, Ygor!," said Frankenstein. "I know he was a friend of yours, but I cannot hide these facts from the Inspector."

Fritz fell silent as Doctor Frankenstein went on, "Yes, he proved untrustworthy, I'm sorry to say. That is why I had to engage this new man, Ygor, from — from the north country."

"I see. Do you know where Fritz is now?"

"I sent him packing. I assume he went to Dunkelhaven. From there I cannot say."

"Thank you so much for this information, doctor. It is most helpful!" said the Inspector, bowing.

"My pleasure," said Doctor Frankenstein, bowing back.

The Inspector turned up his collar against the rain, hurried out and mounted his horse. Doctor Frankenstein waited with steamy impatience while Fritz hobbled out to lock the gate. When he returned, the doctor angrily slammed the front door and bellowed at increasingly ill-fated Fritz.

"You allowed yourself to be *seen*? Truly you are slipping!"

"But, but no one see me — no one except —"

"Except? Except?"

"The cats."

"Oh good Lord, man! Have you quite taken leave of your senses? The *cats?*"

"Yes! They came to there! They follow me, I think. And attack me!"

"What has attacked you is your ever-expanding imagination! Now, we must get back to work! The storm is upon us! The time is now!"

Frankenstein marched for the laboratory door. Fritz limped after him, protesting weakly, "But, Doctor — you has told Inspector Krogh I not me! What kind name is 'Ygor!'"

"The best I could come up with on the spur of the moment! Given the line of his questions, what was I to say? That yes, you stole a brain and assorted bodies at my bidding, and yes, while working in my perfectly benign laboratory, your bungling turned you into this caricature of yourself?

Think, man! On this, the night of nights? Besides, 'Ygor' rather suits you in your current state, don't you think?"

They entered the lab, but "Ygor" quickly closed the door as always. Rolf and Hermann were left, once again, frustrated.

Outside the courtyard wall, Acker, Eckhard and Annalise were equally frustrated. The Inspector's visit had not gotten them any closer to entering the watchtower. They ducked down as the Inspector rode briskly past on his horse, headed back to town.

The horse called to Annalise, "Hmph! The cats are in there! I saw them in the window right above the door! Couldn't have been more obvious. Yet these humans did nothing!"

"Believe me, I share your anguish," grumbled Annalise.

"Upon reaching the stable, I shall unexpectedly bite my master-hr-hr-hr," snorted the horse.

"Please do so," Annalise called after him, then added to herself, "Would that I had a horse's privilege."

Far above them, Rolf and Hermann watched unhappily from the tiny window. "That evil Annalise!" hissed Hermann. "Still she waits outside with her pointlessly cat-hating humans!"

"But again they failed to get in," pointed out Rolf.

"And how long can we count on that?" wailed Hermann.

"Probably not forever," admitted Rolf.

In distant Dunkelhaven, the church bell gonged another hour, tormenting their ears even over the pounding rain. Both cats cringed helplessly, feeling their escape route slipping another notch away.

But inside the lab, work was now at a frenzied pace. "The machines, Ygor! Activate the machines!" commanded Doctor Frankenstein. Curiously, the doctor seemed already to have forgotten Fritz's real name. Resigned to this, Ygor went from machine to machine, pulling levers and throwing knife switches. One by one, the hulking giants roared to life, crackling, sparking, smoking. Doctor Frankenstein feverishly checked gauges and dials; double-checked cables running to the body on the table.

Out in the entry hall, Rolf and Hermann winced at the noise and wrinkled their noses at the acrid smell of ozone. "They're turning on their horrid lightning machines," said Rolf.

"As if there isn't enough lightning outside?" grumbled Hermann.

Just then, the ethereal voice of Father Mouse once again scared the cats half to death, "The ship is still in the harbor." He was on a crossbeam above the window.

"Stop sneaking up on us like that!" yelled Hermann.

"Sorry, Great One. It is in my nature to be quiet," whispered Father Mouse.

There was an awkward silence. Father Mouse was obviously waiting.

"What?" asked Rolf.

"Well, I have made my report, as requested."

"And?"

"And now will you not rid us of the thing, Schmutz, who almost caught me many times on this latest task?"

At this point, Rolf himself was in a mood to eat Father Mouse, but he judged that a leap at the crossbeam would probably end in a painful fall. So he said only, "I remind you, mouse, that even now you only live due to our divine intervention."

"I fail to see the effect of your intervention!" bridled Father Mouse. "I see only myself and my family nearer to death than ever!"

"Do you pretend to question the methods of the gods?" snarled Rolf. Luckily for Rolf (and he did very often seem lucky in this way) a tremendous bolt of lightning struck very near the tower. Shuddering thunder tremored the ancient stone walls. Father Mouse flinched in awe-inspired fear.

In the lab, the bolt had a much different effect, for it was exactly what Doctor Frankenstein was hoping for. His eyes were wild as he shouted, "It is time! Open the skylight, Ygor!"

Ygor shuffled over to a very long chain that extended clear to the roof. He pulled it hand over hand, cranking open the skylight far above. Rain misted down into the room, sizzling on the hot machines.

Out in the hall, Rolf continued his verbal assault on Father Mouse, "I've told you repeatedly that getting rid of the thing, Schmutz, is a complex task. There is much we must know before we can accomplish it." Adding to his annoyance, he found he was having to speak over the sound of the clanking skylight chain coming from the lab, so he ad-libbed, "Like, for instance, what is that annoying noise?"

Father Mouse, frightened, but not thoroughly convinced, answered testily, "It is only the crazy humans opening the roof of that evil room. What has that to do with the thing, Schmutz?"

Rolf and Hermann both perked up visibly. "*Opening* the roof?"

"Yes, some nights they open their big window to the sky." In reality, animals refer to a window as an "invisible mystery wall that frustrates entry and often kills birds." But we'll never get through this story if we get sidetracked by translation issues.

"A window to the sky?" queried Rolf.

"Yes, they open it on stormy nights and let the rain in. We have no idea why."

"Can we reach this sky window?"

"If you go to the house's highest room, there is a rotted hole through which you can reach the roof. You will have to crawl carefully along the roof peaks and ledges, but yes, you can reach the sky window that way."

"Thank you, dear Mouse," enthused Rolf. "This unexpected information could go a long way toward allowing us to rid you of the thing, Schmutz."

"Really?" said Father Mouse, hopefully, relieved that the gods were apparently no longer angry.

"Really," lied Rolf, just as convincingly as Doctor Frankenstein. "Now tell us one last thing. Where is the thing, Schmutz now?"

"Down in the kitchen eating maggot meat."

"Excellent. Come Hermann!"

Rolf and Hermann leapt down from their ledge and set off up the winding stairs. As they padded softly along, Hermann commented, "I will admit, our guileless mouse has been remarkably helpful."

"Won over by my irresistible cunning," smiled Rolf.

"That, and the fact that he has no idea what we are. One could almost feel sorry for him."

"*That* would be a bit of an over reaction."

The top floor of the old watchtower was long vacant, layered in dust and draped in cobwebs. From it they found their way to the highest "room," which was actually the attic, and in there, as the mouse predicted, they found a hole through rotted timbers which led out onto the slate-clad roof. They hopped through it — into the blasting rain.

They studied at the grim path ahead. The roof was a multi-faceted puzzle of slippery, slate-clad peaks, angles, and valleys, made all the more treacherous by the relentless rain. Any misstep could lead to a pell-mell slide ending in 100 foot drop. You may have heard that cats can fall a great distance and not be hurt. This is true up to a certain great distance. Above that, they end up squished just like the rest of us. The roof far exceeded that maximum.

As they eased gingerly forward, Hermann said, "You do note, do you not, my dear Rolf, that we have been wet more than we have been dry in the last few days?"

"I note that we have been wet more than we have been wet in the rest of our *lives*," concurred Rolf.

"Yes, I wanted that to be noted," said Hermann.

"Please," said Rolf nervously, watching each step, "may we concentrate on the task at hand?"

"I'm trying to make conversation so that I may *ignore* the task at hand!" snapped Hermann.

On they went, tremulously picking their way, heading toward the laboratory. It was easy to see where it was, for directly above it, rain drops lit by the lab's electric lights looked like streaking sparks of molten metal.

Inside, Doctor Frankenstein and Ygor were completing the experiment's final step. Working together, they turned the two large hand-cranks that controlled the chains attached to the iron table. It began to rise, carrying the sheet-covered body higher and higher until it disappeared through the open skylight.

So, just as Rolf and Hermann arrived, the table rose into place, completely blocking the skylight opening.

Hermann drew back, "That looks like the table on which they keep their horrible dead thing!"

"More to the point, there is no way into the room from here!" growled Rolf, his whiskers whipping crazily in the wind. "I'll kill that lying mouse!"

"Oh, *now* you agree with me," sulked Hermann, his ears bowed like drooping flowers with the weight of his soaked fur.

But their universe turned blinding white as a multi-forked lightning bolt simultaneously struck four of the copper poles jutting up from the roof. It made Rolf and Hermann's fur shoot straight out so they looked like porcupines.

Down in the lab, Doctor Frankenstein exulted as he watched his electrical gauges leap and bounce with the strike. "That's it! That's it, Ygor! Bring him down! Down!"

Up on the roof, the poles glowed red from the strike. The cats rose shakily to their feet. Steam boiled off them, the wind twisting it into mad curlicues.

Hermann was as angry as Doctor Frankenstein was excited, "Why is he doing this work on a night like this?" he screamed. "Doesn't he know lightning is dangerous?" "Every living thing on *earth* knows lightning is dangerous!"

Then, chains clanking and pulleys squeaking, the table began lowering into the lab.

"Look, look there!" said Rolf. "It's going down! That is our chance! We must jump on!"

Hermann gaped at him, incredulous, "I repeat, dear Rolf, *that looks like the table on which —*"

"I know, Hermann, I know! Even so, we must act! We jump on and ride down into that room, or we stay in this sub-standard town to face Annalise and his deranged cat killers!"

For seemingly long seconds, Hermann stared at the descending table. But at last he said, "Very well. We ride!"

They leaped onto the table and slipped under the sheet covering its cargo. They found they were at the body's feet, so they wriggled forward toward the head, where they'd have more room. Surprisingly, the body was dressed in heavy wool trousers, a worn jacket, and absurdly massive thick-soled boots. Evidently you just didn't leave bodies around naked in those days, even experimental sewn-together ones.

Rolf and Hermann settled on either side of the head. Hermann couldn't help but look at it. It was huge, deathly gray, and crisscrossed with ugly, swollen, freshly-stitched scars. He felt there was only one logical reaction and announced, "Rolf, I am going to arch my back, stick out my soggy fur and go spitting and hissing right out of here!"

"Hermann, please!" begged Rolf. "Not when we are so close to our goal! This dead thing, repellent as it is, cannot hurt you! It can only disgust you."

"Then may I arch and spit in pure disgust?"

"I'd much rather you didn't."

Shuddering, Hermann closed his eyes and shrank back from the sepulchral face as far as he could without falling off the table. "Very well. But I refrain due only to my respect for your opinion, dear Rolf."

"Thank you, my most magnanimous and understanding Hermann." Rolf peeked from beneath the sheet. They were descending slowly toward the floor of the lab. He spotted the gleam of the watch fob, still dangling from Doctor Frankenstein's waistcoat on that same chair, very near where the table must come to rest.

"Dear Hermann, it is within sight! Resist your urges but a moment more!" Hermann closed his eyes tighter and resisted. The table hit the floor with a resounding clang.

"The machines! Shut down the machines!" commanded Doctor Frankenstein. He and Ygor raced around turning off the arcing, sparking machines.

Rolf saw his chance! Quick as, well, lightning, he shot from beneath the sheet, bounded to the waistcoat and snagged the watch chain in his teeth.

Peering from under the sheet, Hermann watched with excitement, paws resting on the head of the body, which he'd forgotten for the moment.

Until, literally under his nose, *the "dead" body's eyes opened!*

Hermann stared down into the filmy yellow orbs, his own eyes goggling in disbelief. His tail curled. He back arched. His fur rose.

Rolf dove back under the sheet, grinning broadly with the watch dangling under his chin.

"I've done it, Hermann!" he exulted. Then he saw that Hermann did not share his exultation. "Whatever is the matter with you? Stop shaking! Stop arching! We've won!"

He could see Hermann was about to hiss and spit with wild abandon, so, yet again, he clamped his paws over Hermann's mouth and tried to make him stop shaking.

As Ygor and Doctor Frankenstein rushed back to the table, Ygor noticed the sheet moving. He pointed it out excitedly, "Doctor Fronshtein! He moves!"

The body's right hand had slid from under the sheet. Doctor Frankenstein grabbed it to feel for a pulse. His own hand was actually brushing against shuddering Rolf's butt, not that the excited doctor would have noticed. Meanwhile, Hermann had had enough. He batted Rolf's paws aside so that he could hiss-whisper: "T-t-t-t-the dead thing is aliiiiiiiive!"

"What?!" cried Rolf. But at that same instant Doctor Frankenstein shouted in triumph, "It's alive! Alive! Aliiiiiiiiive!"

The cats flinched and ducked even lower, "What is he shouting about?" wailed Hermann. "Doesn't he even see that this morbid thing is *alive*?"

But Rolf, for once, had nothing to say, for he now saw what Hermann had seen, the sulfur-yellow eyes of the huge being — looking right at him.

Rolf stared. Hermann trembled. They even forgot to be worried about being discovered. But they were safe for the moment because, instead of lifting the sheet, Doctor Frankenstein tugged Ygor to the head of the table. "Come, come! We must stand him up! Let his first view of the world be that of an upright man!"

"Yes, Doctor!"

They turned cranks beneath the table, tilting it swiftly up toward vertical.

Under the sheet, the paralyzed cats were taken by surprise. They slid down the slick metal surface. The watch, hanging from Rolf's mouth, caught in the breast pocket of the old jacket the body was wearing. Watch and chain were yanked from his teeth as he and Hermann slid off the foot of the table.

Unseen by the doctor and Ygor, who were behind the now upright table, they quickly hid behind one of the machines.

"Curses and double curses," cursed Rolf. I've lost the tick-tock *again!*"

Hermann was still overwhelmed by the sight of the body awakening. "Alive! Alive! Aliiiiive!" he wheezed.

Doctor Frankenstein yanked the sheet off, revealing at last the thing on the table — the Monster! Now, we're going to stick with convention and refer to Doctor Frankenstein's creation as "The Monster," since that's what people expect. However, you'll discover, as we continue to present the real facts of this totally true report, that it is hardly a fair moniker for the poor guy.

Anyway, Doctor F. yanked off the sheet and —

Hermann gaped.

Rolf gaped.

Even Ygor gaped. He hadn't really paid that much attention to the gruesome assembly part of the job, preferring not to watch. But this giant, covered with red-and-black-and blue, puss-oozing scars, was indeed a terrible sight.

Doctor Frankenstein, however, remained delighted beyond measure. He quickly undid the straps holding the Monster to the table, gently letting him down on his feet. Then he stepped in front of his creation, stood up proudly and announced, "Greetings! Welcome back to existence! I am Doctor Frankenstein, and I have given you — life!"

The Monster stared blankly at him with not the slightest hint of comprehension.

"You are somewhat confused, of course," said the doctor. "Let us begin slowly." He raised his hand, holding up two fingers. "Here, you see my hand, do you not? How many fingers am I holding up?"

The Monster followed the movement of Doctor Frankenstein's hand, but only emitted a low growl, "Raaarh."

Flustered, the doctor tried something else, "Well then, can you mimic my actions? Can you raise your arms like this?"

He held his arms akimbo, as they used to say. The Monster did nothing. Worried, Doctor Frankenstein whispered to Ygor, "He does not seem to understand anything."

Ygor, of course, knew what the reason might be — a certain abnormal brain — but he was not about to admit it. Instead he offered an explanation he hoped the doctor might accept, "Maybe surprise, to be 'live suddenly. Think maybe he only need some time."

"Yes, yes," said Frankenstein hopefully, then remembering, "Oh! The time! I must note the time of this momentous occasion!" He turned to the Monster, speaking loudly and slowly as though to someone deaf, "I'm going to make some notes. Just wait here and — and relax."

He snatched up a pencil and paper, then raced behind the upright table to the chair where his waistcoat hung. Ygor just backed away from the imposing Monster, wringing his hands with worry.

Nearby, Rolf and Hermann watched, and Rolf assessed the situation, eyeing the pocket on the Monster's jacket, where he knew the watch was hidden, "We must snatch the tick-tock again!"

"From the giant formerly dead human?!" squeaked Hermann.

"What choice do we have? Now look, look there," Rolf pointed up through the criss-crossing cables and beams above them. "The sky window is still open. If we leap and climb like true cats should, we can escape that way!"

"But the giant formerly dead human is so gigantic — so ugly — so —"

"Stop it! It is like any other human, or mostly human, or formerly human. That is, it is *slow*! We shall leap together. One of us is sure to snag the tick-tock's chain with our claws. Then we'll race up the wooden beams and right out the sky window, and then it's off to Pago-Pago!"

Hermann sadly nodded his assent. With Rolf leading the way, they scuttled from one hiding spot to the next, moving in on their target.

But in his earnestness, Rolf had forgotten about Ygor, who was behind them. When he saw them, he very quickly went from astonished to extremely vengeful. Quietly snatching up the iron poker from the incinerator, he sneaked toward the cats even as they sneaked toward the

Monster.

Over behind the tilted-up table, Doctor Frankenstein called, "Ygor! Where in Heaven's name is my watch? It was right here, wasn't it?"

Ygor didn't answer. He was triumphantly raising the poker to strike! But at that moment, the cats leapt on the Monster.

Rolf had always been a bit more accurate than Hermann. He hit the Monster squarely in the chest, pawing at the pocket. Hermann, driven by fear, exceeded his expectations and went high, slamming directly into the Monster's face, digging in his claws.

The Monster unleashed a roar that rattled every beaker and test tube in the lab. "Raaaaaaarh!" With surprising speed, he grabbed both Rolf and Hermann, plucked them off and flung them straight up like cat missiles.

Thus, they *did* leave by way of the "sky window," just not in the manner they had intended. They arced into the stormy sky, landed on the wet, wind-swept slate roof, slid and clawed and scrabbled and *barely* caught themselves on the very edge, dizzily high above the stone courtyard.

Back inside, Doctor Frankenstein, startled by the noise, stepped from behind the table to see the Monster roaring in anger, and Ygor with up-raised poker, poised to strike.

"Ygor! What on Earth are you doing? My ultimate masterpiece is but a minute old and you torment it?"

Ygor instantly dropped the poker, which clanged to the floor in an embarrassingly loud way. Then he pointed meekly upward, "It was — the cats," he whimpered.

The Monster roared again, rubbing his scratched face and lurching unsteadily around the lab. Doctor Frankenstein snarled at Ygor, "Worthless idiot! I should have turned you in to the Inspector!"

"No, Doctor, please! It was —"

"Stop! I'll hear none of your nonsense! Just — just help me get him below. We'll lock him in one of the old cells. I can only hope that, given some time, he'll improve."

They edged nervously toward the Monster. Gingerly, each man took hold of one massive hand and tugged. He calmed a little, and let them lead him out.

On the roof, in the drenching rain, Rolf and Hermann retraced the difficult route back to the hole in the attic, slipped inside and flopped down among the web-covered timbers.

Then, everybody got a good night's sleep. Except for Rolf and Hermann, who heard Schmutz patrolling on the floors below and worried he would find them. And except for Ygor, who worried that Doctor Frankenstein would find out about the less-desirable brain. And except for Doctor Frankenstein, who worried that he had meddled with forces with which man was not meant to meddle. And except for Acker and Eckhard, who worried that the diamond cat would yet escape them. And except for Annalise, who worried that her masters would beat her if she let the cats escape. And except for the mouse family, because mice worry all the time and never sleep soundly. Okay, actually only Schmutz got a good night's sleep, once done patrolling. His life was lonely, but pretty worry-free.

CHAPTER THIRTEEN

Rolf woke to Hermann groaning. He looked around and saw that his partner had moved as far away as possible into a corner of the attic and was hunched up behind a beam.

"Hermann? Are you all right?"

"No. If I must repeat it, I'm quite — stopped up. I am still unable to complete my kitty business."

"Well, events have been stressful."

"I maintain that my distress is caused by that last piece of fish."

Rolf rose and stretched, first forelegs then back. Soon, Hermann waddled over and sat, grim-faced.

Rolf asked, "You have given up?"

"Yes. Again. For I am sure you will soon say we must find the hideous human who only recently was dead and risk our lives to get the tick-tock."

Rolf was taken aback, "Why yes, Hermann. I was just about to suggest that. You are uncharacteristically focused this morning."

"When there is only one option, and it is dire at best, it is hard to forget it."

Hearing no sign of the thing, Schmutz, they dropped softly from the attic into the abandoned top floor hallway. They sniffed the air, and picked up the faintest scent of the Monster. There was no mistaking it — a most distinctive blend of moldy cloth, injured flesh, nose-burning ozone — and an unsettling hint of death. It came from somewhere far below.

Hermann said, with dread, "Now we must go down the many flights of stairs, all the while in fear of meeting the thing, Schmutz."

Rolf thought that, then said, "Only one floor below is the hole in the wall by which we first escaped the thing. We could leap into it and repeat our frightening but highly effective fall to the bottom of this stone house."

Hermann's head and ears drooped, "Of course, plummet again down the evil black hole of soot. Why not? Genius, Rolf."

"Thank you, Hermann, said Rolf, taking the compliment as legitimate.

And so they executed the suggestion. Slipping softly down to the floor on which were located Doctor Frankenstein's and Ygor's bedrooms, they dashed down the hall, jumped up into the chimney clean-out and again, but rather more gracefully this time, slid-fell to the lowest level of the tower.

Once in the ash chamber, they climbed the wooden ladder to the floor above, the one with the dark, branching hallways. And then stopped, ears, tails and noses high.

"What luck! He is down here somewhere!" said Rolf excitedly, for the scent of the Monster was quite strong.

"Our luck astounds," said Hermann flatly.

They sniffed again, choosing the hall from which the scent wafted. Hugging the walls, stepping ever so cautiously, they followed it.

The hall was long, but curved. They couldn't see far ahead. As they went, they passed small dismal rooms with barred doors. They were in the watchtower's dungeon, where countless prisoners, some innocent, some guilty, had suffered untold misery over the centuries. But since Rolf and Hermann didn't know that, they didn't care at all. They moved on, side-by-side, in cat lock-step, trying to zero in on the smell.

Then they heard the awful click-scrape of the deformed claws belonging to the thing, Schmutz. It was just beyond the curve ahead, coming toward them!

"Run!" hissed Hermann.

"No, jump!" whispered Rolf, and he leapt almost straight up, balancing on a sconce high on the wall. Hermann followed suit, springing to a sconce on the opposite side. Fortunately, the sconces, which held torches to light the hallway, were not lit.

The thing, Schmutz, lumbered around the bend. Rolf and Hermann literally held their breath as the hulking creature passed slowly beneath them.

As Hermann stared down at the beast, he noted that its bare, wrinkled skin was zigzagged with jagged scars and stitches. This gave him a very unwelcome revelation.

Rolf saw Hermann's eyes bugging out, but assumed it was simply because Hermann was terrified as always. They continued holding their breath until, at last, the thing, Schmutz, passed out of sight.

Rolf leapt to the floor, "Come on, quickly."

But Hermann seemed glued to his sconce, "Rolf, did you see? Did you see?"

"See what?"

The awful scars all over the back of the thing, Schmutz!"

"I was busy holding my breath, now come on."

But Hermann rattled on, "Don't you realize what that implies, taken together with its mutilated ears, its hairless tail, its mismatched eyes, its out-of-place cat paws, and its variegated skin colors?"

Rolf did not get the implication at all. With some impatience, he said, "It is a pitiable yet still intimidating animal. We know this. What of it?"

"Rolf! I think it is a c-c-cat!"

"What?! Don't be ridiculous! No cat would ever, *could* ever, sink to such a state!"

"Not willingly, no!" Hermann babbled. "But, do you not remember what the little mouse said? That the human 'made' the thing, Schmutz? I think it is true!"

"Hermann! The mouse is un-educated and extremely naïve!"

"Perhaps, but think, Rolf. Have you ever seen a thing such as the thing, Schmutz?"

"I have not, but no animal gets *made*. All of them, even absurdly ugly ones, get born, you know, the natural way."

"I think that is true in any place *outside* this wretched house of death," said Hermann with gravity. Remember the jars of — of unmentionable *parts* in the room of lightning? I tell you, Rolf, that crazed human *made* the thing, Schmutz! Made it just as he made his abominable no-longer-dead human!"

Rolf was now a bit incensed, because cats have a built-in sense of decorum and superiority about cats in general. "Hermann! The thing, Schmutz is not a cat! It cannot be! And you are, with your more than usually annoying raving, deterring us once again from our utmost and important goal! Now will you *please* come on!"

But Hermann remained on his sconce, analyzing his disturbing theory. And as he analyzed, he began to sink down. This was not by design, for *he* was not moving. The sconce was moving. And as things often turn out in places like the watchtower, the sconce proved to be a disguised lever that opened a hidden door in the wall, revealing a secret passage.

Rolf stared at the suddenly appeared opening, *"Now* what have you done, Hermann?"

"Nothing!" Hermann nodded at the sconce, "This thing moved without warning!"

But then they both noticed the odor of the Monster wafting from the passage — stronger than ever.

"He is through there somewhere!" exclaimed Rolf. "Bravo, Hermann! You've discovered a short cut!"

"My pleasure, Rolf." Hermann was always happy to have done something Rolf approved of. He leapt down and they entered the dark passage.

As it happened, neither Doctor Frankenstein nor Ygor knew about the hidden door. In fact, no human living knew about it. It accessed a whole network of passages intended for moving high profile dignitaries, or high profile prisoners, from cell to cell in secret. Hence the name, "secret passage."

These low, narrow tunnels meandered behind the cells of the dungeon. Occasionally, Rolf and Hermann had to jump on other sconces to open doors into intersecting tunnels. They could find the hidden doors by sniffing for subtle drafts of air wafting through almost invisible cracks around the door edges.

"Rather exciting, isn't it?" said Rolf, "Opening doors like humans do!"

Door-opening was, of course, normally impossible for cats.

"Yes," said Hermann, still unenthusiastic.

"My dear Hermann, I fear your intestinal woes have dulled you to the enjoyment of the moment."

"The moment leads inexorably to a meeting with the no-longer-dead human."

Rolf refused to be discouraged. He merrily leaped on another sconce. To their surprise, the door it controlled opened through an outer wall into a secluded corner of the courtyard.

"More good fortune!" declared Rolf. "The perfect escape route when we have achieved our goal."

"Huzzah, Rolf. Huzzah."

"Hermann, I mean, really!" They left the door open and continued along the tunnel.

While we pause outside, however, we should point out what Acker and Eckhard were up to just then. Having failed to rile the townsfolk into a mob, and having been disappointed in Inspector Krogh's timid treatment of Doctor Frankenstein, they'd sunk into a dark mood.

Increasingly worried that the diamond-swallowing cat would soon divest itself of same via normal kitty business, they had come up with a rather more severe plan. Searching the surrounding woods, they had availed themselves of some heavy clubs and now lay in wait at the gate. They intended to attack either Ygor or Doctor Frankenstein — whoever came out first — steal that person's keys, and use them to enter the watchtower.

And while we're talking about what others were doing, we must note that Ygor was heading down the stairs to the dungeon carrying a tray. On it was a breakfast of eggs and cured ham which he had cooked for the Monster. He had chosen the best ham they had on hand, because he felt sorry for the creature. This seemingly harmless choice, like many in this adventure, would have a significant impact on upcoming events.

Dr. Frankenstein and Ygor had put the Monster in the dungeon's largest cell. A single torch burned in a wall sconce beside the barred cell door, lighting only a small area of the irregularly shaped room. Moss decorated the stone walls. Somewhere water dripped with a melancholy echo.

Across from the door, lit dimly by the flickering orange torch light, the Monster sat on a pile of damp straw, leaning despondently against the wall. He looked up as a key rattled in the door's lock and Ygor entered with the tray. The Monster gazed vacantly at him, seeming lost and dejected. Ygor felt sad as he set the tray on a small wooden table and gestured to it. But the Monster did not move.

Ygor hesitated, then spoke softly in his new dialect, "I not know if you understand me, but if do, want to say I sorry. Sorry for bringing you sad brain here and have Doctor Fronshtein wake it up. Sorry for lock you in here, too."

The Monster did not respond. Ygor did not know if it understood him or not, and we don't know, either. So, Ygor sighed and went back out, locking the door.

Neither he nor the Monster knew that there were actually two doors into the cell. The other was a secret one, hidden in an alcove at one end.

Rolf and Hermann, still searching the passages, had just arrived at that very door. Rolf sniffed cautiously around its edges, and was elated, "The smell is strong! That's him! I'm sure of it!"

Hermann sniffed and, surprisingly, was elated also. "That's ham! I'm sure of it!"

"What?"

"Fresh cooked ham! Can't you smell it?"

"Hermann, only moments ago you seemed fully engaged in our primary task. Now —"

"Rolf!" Hermann interrupted, "I suffer from a significant sparseness of sustenance!"

"We are *both* hungry, dear friend. I only suggest that for now we prioritize —"

Ignoring him, Hermann eagerly leapt on a wall sconce. The secret door quietly opened.

They peered into the cell. From the alcove, they could see only the wooden table with the tray of eggs and ham. It steamed invitingly.

"Food!" whispered Hermann and, fear completely forgotten, he rushed to the table, leapt up, and began gobbling.

Rolf sighed resignedly. He was about to follow when he heard an ominous noise. An immense shadow fell across the wall behind Hermann — and the Monster stepped into view.

The Monster stared at Hermann. He had logged only a few memories so far, but one of them involved this cat, and it was not a pleasant one. His already scary face crinkled into an even more terrifying mask of anger. He stepped softly forward, huge hands stretching out toward oblivious Hermann.

Rolf, to his credit, did not delay. Ears flat, fur spiked, he launched himself out of the alcove with a loud yowl. If you've ever heard angry cats fight, you know they can make *very* loud sounds. Today Rolf was the essence of demonic cat fury.

The Monster was just passing the torch on the wall when Rolf exploded into view. Startled, he stepped back, accidentally pressing his shoulder against the flame. With a roar, he jerked away from the pain, knocking the torch from the sconce. It fell into the straw on the cell floor.

Now even more furious, the Monster charged Hermann. But Hermann had by now noticed he was in big trouble. He bounded off the table just before the Monster's fist slammed down and turned it into toothpicks. Then he and Rolf zigzagged desperately around the cell, trying to angle past the Monster to the alcove.

Ygor, alarmed at the roaring of the Monster, had hurried back and now looked in through the bars of the door. He was dumbfounded to see the cats, those same hated cats, circling madly around the Monster. Even worse, the fallen torch had set the straw ablaze! Ygor jammed his key into the lock, kicked open the door, snatched up the torch and stamped vigorously on the flaming straw to put it out.

Rolf and Hermann, meanwhile, executed a flawless double-back, ran right between the Monster's legs, and zipped across the cell to disappear into the alcove.

The Monster whirled, searching for them, but all he saw was Ygor — holding the torch. The Monster felt his burned shoulder, and stared at Ygor some more, his yellow eyes narrowing, his scarred brow furrowing.

Ygor looked from the Monster's smoldering jacket to the torch. With a soft moan, he realized what the Monster thought.

"No — I not hurt you. It was the —" he began.

But the Monster stretched out his powerful arms and stalked toward Ygor with his trademark sound, the low and sinister, "Raaarh." Ygor backed away, brandishing the torch, "No! You go back!"

The angry Monster kept coming, growling louder. Ygor swung the torch wildly as he staggered backward toward the cell door.

"Stop! Keep away!"

At that moment, Doctor Frankenstein burst in. "What is all this noise?" he demanded. "What is happening down here?"

He took in the tableau before him: his creation, clearly angry, reaching for Ygor, who was waving a torch in its face.

"Are you mad, man?" yelled Doctor Frankenstein. "You can think of nothing more pressing to do than come down here and torment this sad creature?!"

The Monster paused, startled by the newcomer's outburst. Ygor scuttled over to join Doctor Frankenstein, trying to explain.

"No, no, Fronshtein! I only feed him, just as you say to! It was — was —" But he glanced around the cell and saw no sign of Hermann and Rolf. He could not bring himself to speak the truth. "I afraid of him," he lied softly.

"Afraid? Afraid of a wretched thing not even a day old? That can't even speak?" fumed Doctor Frankenstein. "Out! Out of here immediately! Oh, leave it alone! Leave it alone!"

"Yes, Fronshtein," mumbled Ygor. He hurriedly returned the torch to its sconce and followed the doctor out, locking the door.

The Monster, left alone, now thought again of the cats. Twice they had tormented him! And they were here somewhere. He growled, and slowly turned, searching.

Rolf and Hermann had paused in the alcove. Now they grew tense. It was always obvious when a human was aware of them, even a never-before-heard-of, formerly-dead human.

"Rolf," whispered Hermann, "I do hope you'll agree that we should run. That we should await a better time to snatch the tick-tock."

The Monster's shadow fell over them. He was staring into the dark alcove, but couldn't quite see them — yet. Rolf's voice shook a little, "I do agree, dear Hermann."

The secret door was still open. The cats darted into the passage beyond. They heard a snarl that told them their sudden movement had been seen. But they did not look back. When you're a cat at maximum escape velocity, you don't look back. Your ears tell what's behind you, and their ears said a huge insanely scary thing was thundering after them with intent to kill.

As they careened along the twisting tunnels, Rolf remembered the exit they'd accidentally opened into the courtyard. Since cats are rarely lost, even in mazes, he made all the right turns to take them right to it.

They flew out into the courtyard. Beside the exit was a scraggly tree hugging the watchtower wall. They scampered up it and hid in the spring foliage just before the Monster stomped out of the passage.

He stopped short and looked around, surprised to find himself outside. Ironically, Rolf and Hermann had led him out of the confusing tunnels where he might otherwise have been lost for hours. Just a few feet above his head, the two cats clung to branches in trembling terror. They knew, if he looked up, they were dead.

Compounding our ever-increasing ironies however, it was Annalise who prevented that possible outcome. Instantly aware that Rolf and Hermann were nearby, she set up a howl outside the gate. Hearing her, the Monster turned to see the gate, noting that it led out of the courtyard. Since the only people he'd met so far had locked him in a cell ten minutes after he woke up, it must have seemed like a good idea to get away from them, because he headed straight for the gate.

Outside, Acker and Eckhard had jumped up as soon as Annalise started barking. Hiding in the brush, they were excited to hear footsteps coming toward the gate. They raised their cudgels, eager to attack whoever unlocked it.

But the gate was not unlocked. It was *smashed open* with the shriek of uprooted hinge pins. There, framed in its remnants, stood neither Doctor

Frankenstein nor Ygor/Fritz. There stood a seven foot tall, yellow-eyed, gray-skinned, multiply-scarred *monster!*

Annalise's bark choked off in a strangled squeak. Acker's club fell from his limp hands. But Eckhard had already started a powerful swing with his club. He stumbled forward in the effort to stop himself, falling on his knees as his club clattered across the cobblestones.

"Begging your pardon, sir!" he stammered.

The Monster stared at them, uncomprehending. The world was no doubt pretty confusing to his messed-up brain. Then he stalked right past them toward Dunkelhaven.

The trio watched, open-mouthed.

"What — was — *that?*" asked Acker.

"I — don't — know," replied Eckhard. "But, but did you see its hand?"

"Its hand? Are you mad? What care I about its hand?"

"It had a tattoo of a cat — just like Dedrick's!"

"Well, there's not much I understand right now, but I can tell you that was *not* Dedrick!" Acker sank down beside fallen Eckhard, adding, "Why are the fates so cruel? Why did those hated cats have to come here of all places?"

Meanwhile, up in the tree, said cats assessed this latest development. "The no-longer-dead human with the tick-tock is getting away," Hermann pointed out.

"Indeed he is," said Rolf. "However, as you can hear, Annalise and her hated owners are still outside the gate. We must go out the other way."

"Not the *other* way!" cried Hermann.

"There *is* no other way!"

"Oh, very well!" snapped Hermann.

Rolf leapt down, intending to retrace their route through the various secret passages and hallways to the kitchen so they could exit, once again, through the sewer.

No sooner had he entered the passage when he skidded to a halt. Hermann ran headlong, and rather unceremoniously, into his butt.

"Why do you stop? We must hurry, must we not?" asked Hermann.

Uncharacteristically, Rolf did not answer. Hermann quickly saw the reason why.

Two mismatched eyes glowered at them from deeper in the dark passage.

It was the thing, Schmutz.

Rolf about-faced, right over Hermann, and bounded up the tree. Hermann attempted the same maneuver, but just before he made the jump to the tree trunk, a fur-splotched paw slammed down on his tail.

He was caught! He looked over his shoulder at the face of the thing, Schmutz. Its irregular, fleshy lips curled back from its snaggly teeth.

Up in the tree, Rolf was horrified! Sensing that cruel destiny had dealt them their last hand, he crouched, intending to leap onto the back of the devilish thing. He knew with cat certainty that it would be a suicide attack but, while Rolf was in many ways vain and self-serving, he valued his friendship with Hermann above all else.

But Hermann, to Rolf's utter astonishment, acted on his own intuition. Suddenly adopting a cheery, nonchalant attitude, he *spoke to the thing!*

"Hello, brother cat!" he said, in cat.

Schmutz was quite taken aback. His lips paused in mid-curl. There was a tense pause. Then he said hesitantly, "Er, hello?" His voice was creepy and gurgly — but clearly was, or once had been, a cat voice.

Rolf, rooted to his branch in mid-crouch, was thunderstruck. He thought to himself, *Hermann was right. The thing is a cat!* At the same instant, he saw Hermann shoot him an I-told-you-so look.

All the while, Schmutz stared at Hermann in amazement, "You is — cat?"

"Of course! We're both cats!" said Hermann, cheerily. "Brothers! Soul mates! I'm exactly like you — more or less."

"Why you be here in my lonely house," asked Schmutz.

Hermann said, "Well, we, my companion and I, we're here on a sort of a mission, you see, and it involves that very large no-longer-dead human. You know about him, don't you?"

"Yes," said Schmutz softly. "No-longer-dead. Like me."

Hermann smugly fired a second I-told-you-so look at Rolf. His theory about Schmutz was fully verified! Then he boldly carried on, "Yes! That one. Like you. Well, you know, he has a tick-tock. And we wish to get it."

"Cats want tick-tock?" mused Schmutz. "Why? Can't eat."

"True, so very true. You are so correct, my brother and friend and very similar-to-me cat." Hermann felt he was doing quite well and saw no reason to lie, so he plunged ahead with the truth, "The thing is, there is a ship down in the harbor. You can just see its sails from the top of this tall house. Have you noticed? Never mind, it doesn't matter. The point is, soon that ship's bell will begin to ring, announcing that it is ready to sail, and we hope to be on it, Rolf and I. But we must give that tick-tock to a certain pack rat first, so that he will let us get onto the ship. Then we will sail away to a place we have heard of called Pago-Pago, where all cats are treated nicely."

"Cats treated nice? Seem very strange," said Schmutz dubiously. Being treated nicely was outside his experience.

"Well, these are strange times, are they not?" vamped Hermann.

Schmutz had to agree with that. Life had been pretty much non-stop strange for him since he had awakened on Doctor Frankenstein's metal table.

Up in the tree, Rolf watched, fascinated. He had never seen Hermann so brilliant. Then he noticed a slight movement in the watchtower wall beside his tree branch. It was the mouse family, crowded together in a gap between two stones, staring out at him.

Mother mouse pointed downward with her tail and noted in a chiding tone, "The thing, Schmutz is still here."

"Silence!" commanded Rolf, with as much regal imperiousness as he could. "My colleague is casting a most important spell on the thing even now!" And he hoped that were true.

Down below, Hermann was rattling on, "Anyway, since the no-longer-dead human has left this place —"

"My lonely house," interrupted Schmutz.

"Exactly, since he has left your lonely house, we have no need to stay. So we'll just be running along to catch up to him, you see?"

Schmutz gave out a long, resigned sigh and said, rather unexpectedly,

"No."

"No?" said Hermann.

"No. Must now kill and eat you," said Schmutz.

"B-beg p-pardon?" stammered Hermann.

"If not kill and eat trespassers, not get food," explained Schmutz. "Only job."

"But — but surely you can make this one exception for *me*, your brother, friend, soul mate and reasonably similar kindred spirit!"

"Not know word 'kindred,'" said Schmutz.

"Oh, *feathers*! It means the same as all the other words! Look at it in context!" cried Hermann. He strained to pull his tail free of Schmutz's powerful paw, but could not.

Up above, Mother Mouse scoffed to Rolf, "Great gods from outdoors, are you? I think the thing, Schmutz is about to eat your partner!"

"Because — because you have not completed your tasks!" blurted Rolf.

"No more tasks!" snarled Mother Mouse.

Rolf was astonished that something so small could snarl so convincingly, but he forced himself to stay on track, to try to come up with some plan, and quickly said, "But you've helped us a great deal. We have learned much. We — we have discovered the thing's weakness."

Father Mouse could not help being curious. He pushed forward beside Mother Mouse, "You have?"

"Don't listen," growled Mother Mouse. "He is lying."

"No, no!" lied Rolf. "His weakness is — is that if he leaves this house, we can cast a spell that will drive him out forever!"

"So, cast it!" demanded Mother Mouse.

Rolf now had a sudden stroke of genius. Truth be told, he felt he had them rather often, but this one seemed particularly good: if he could get the mice to run out the gate, and if Schmutz chased them, Annalise and his humans might also be distracted long enough for Rolf and Hermann to escape unnoticed. But, he had to convince the mice.

So he began, "We can't cast the spell unless the thing, Schmutz leaves this house. Don't you see? This is your last and greatest and most important task!"

"No!" declared Mother Mouse. "No more!"

"You must! I'm sorry, but you must make the thing, Schmutz chase you one last time. It must be the grandest chase ever to — to —"

He glanced wildly out the destroyed courtyard gate, looking for some destination, any destination. In the seemingly interminable pause, Father Mouse asked impatiently, "To where?"

Rolf's eye fell on the majestic old windmill across the valley. "To there!" he said, "To the old mill!" (In case you're wondering, the actual animal phrase for "the old mill" is "strange-smelling human house with arms that move and that makes frightening noises," but we promised we weren't going to get waylaid by this sort of thing, so this is really, really the last time we'll bring it up.)

"No!" squeaked Mother Mouse again, "It is too far! The thing, Schmutz will catch us most certainly!"

Even Father Mouse resisted, "You ask us to leave our home of homes? The only place we mouse-kind have lived for all of time?"

"You must!" pleaded Rolf. "This is the final challenge! You must make the thing, Schmutz chase you away from your home of homes, that we may cast the final spell, the spell that will keep him away forever!"

"But we have never been beyond these walls!" wailed Mother Mouse. "How will we know what to do? And if we live, how will we know you have cast the spell?"

Rolf pawed his face with frustration. Idiotic mouse questions! But he kept calm — and continued lying, "You will see an angel. She will appear as a light from — above — from the heavens! Then you will know it is safe to return and that the thing, Schmutz cannot follow you."

Mother and Father Mouse looked into each others' beady eyes. Could it be true? Could they hope to be at last rid of the thing, Schmutz?

"I'll do it, oh Tall-eared Divinity!" announced Father Mouse suddenly.

"*We'll* do it!" said Mother Mouse. "We'll all live or die together, husband!" She called to her little ones. They piled onto her like tiny pink flower buds.

Mother Mouse and Father Mouse scampered down the stone wall to the courtyard. Taking their mission quite literally, they boldly bolted right under Schmutz's dripping jaws, then raced for the gate.

Schmutz, already conflicted about eating Hermann, was probably glad for the distraction. He gurgle-growled and said, "Ooooh, the mice! *Hate* the mice! Can't never catch!" And he bounded after them. Hermann, who had been pulling madly on his pinned tail all this time, flew right over backward as Schmutz galloped off.

Rolf dropped lightly down beside over-turned Hermann, pushed his nose under him and flipped him upright. Hermann took a moment to stroke his ruffled fur as he said, "'An angel will appear as a light from the heavens?!' Where did you invent *that* idea?"

"Just popped into my head. They were being obstinate and it was clear they needed to hear something impressive."

Outside the gate, Annalise was startled to see a whole mouse family streak past her. Barely had she gotten over that surprise when the thing, Schmutz, rounded the corner and came at her, snorting and drooling.

Now understand, Annalise was a brave dog. Under normal circumstances, if she had to, she could fight as well as most males. But this — this *thing* now hulking toward her was hardly normal. With a piteous, puppy-like yelp, she sprang sideways out of Schmutz's path, straining desperately at her leash.

Mother Mouse was lagging behind Father Mouse. She was on rough, unfamiliar ground and was burdened by her babies. Schmutz's glistening snout was an inch from her behind, and she was a split second from doomed.

A short distance beyond Annalise, Acker and Eckhard were unaware of the chase drama, as they were still arguing about the previous drama.

"If I am to stay in this place," railed rattled Eckhard, "I'll thank you to tell me what that was!"

"You saw as good as me!" retorted Acker. "It was both more and less than a man! Some abomination!"

"An abomination with Dedrick's tattoo!" cried Eckhard.

Acker was going to re-state his position that the Monster in no way resembled the late Dedrick. But, at that instant, Mother Mouse scooted between his legs. This saved her.

The seventy-five pound Schmutz (have we mentioned he weighed seventy-five pounds?) piled into Acker at knee height. He and the cat-monster tumbled together in an avalanche of flailing limbs. Schmutz rose first, snarling wetly in Acker's face, then tore off after the mice.

A nearly paralyzed Eckhard pointed after the second monster they had seen this day.

"What — was — *that?*" asked Eckhard.

"I — don't — know!" replied Acker.

Eckhard sank to his knees, "I'm sad to admit it, partner in theft, but I am afraid. The lure of the diamond is losing its hold over me."

"I understand," said Acker, getting shakily to his feet, "But I'll now suggest a path that don't require hardly nothing of us."

"Which would be?"

"Which would be that we fly to the town and tell that wretched Inspector Krogh what we have seen here now with our own eyes. And demand that he return and do some justice!"

"Flying from here is a welcome thought! Let us fly at once."

And they did. Annalise did not resist the tug of the leash. She, too, was so rattled by what she'd seen that she was willing to forget The Hated Rolf and Hermann for the moment.

To pile on a bit more irony, those very cats were even now watching her from the top of the courtyard wall. "Even better than I had hoped," said Rolf. "Annalise and her humans have fled at the very sight of the various monsters in this awful place."

"Genius, Rolf." And this time Hermann was not being sarcastic.

So, quite relaxed for a change, they paused to observe the astonishing chase — the mice and the thing, Schmutz — playing out across the valley below. With their years of experience in mouse chasing, they were agog at the mouse family's extraordinary skill.

Hermann marveled, "Look at them twist and turn! So fast! So precise!"

Rolf added, "Oh and see there how they doubled back! Schmutz literally tripped over himself!"

They continued to watch in amazement as the mice dodged, and ducked, and practically cart-wheeled, staying inches ahead of Schmutz as they headed steadily toward the old windmill. Finally, pursued and pursuer were lost from view.

After a quiet moment, Hermann said, "It would be an honor to catch mice such as those."

"It would indeed," nodded Rolf.

Rolf prepared to jump down from the wall. But he sensed Hermann was hanging back.

"What is it, friend?" he asked.

"I — I am feeling something," said Hermann.

"Yes?"

"It is not pleasant."

"Your intestinal troubles."

"No, it's elsewhere." He pointed a paw at his heart. "I'm feeling — guilty."

It was a word neither Rolf nor Hermann had ever used.

"What?" said Rolf.

"I feel we have, what is the word — betrayed these mice," said Hermann softly.

"Betrayed *mice?*" scoffed Rolf. "Now you are annoying me. Whatever do you mean? Until now you have thought of nothing but eating them!"

"I know, I know. But this unique circumstance has begun to prey on my mind. Outside their world, mice know cats. Cats know mice. When we encounter one another, we all know the rules. But these mice don't know what we are. And now will probably die doing our bidding."

"But, but —" spluttered Rolf, "that is all to *our* benefit."

"Yes, yes, and that is as it should be, of course, but, all the same, it makes me feel guilty. They've done what they've done because they believed in us. Trusted us."

Rolf was silent for a long time. Finally he said, "Well, this is certainly unpleasant. Now you've made *me* feel guilty. And I'm sure I've never felt that way before."

"I'm sorry."

"You should be. Because there is no point to it. There is nothing we can do about it. We have to find that no-longer-dead human, get that tick-tock, and get out of here, or — or the mice will have died for nothing!"

While Rolf and Hermann were dealing with a new and confounding emotion, Doctor Frankenstein and Ygor were facing and equally confounding problem. They had just discovered that the star of the doctor's miracle experiment was missing.

They were standing outside the Monster's empty cell, its door still securely bolted. Then Doctor Frankenstein glared at Ygor, "You've let him escape, you imbecile!"

Ygor gestured helplessly to the still-bolted door, "But za door — you see me lock it!"

"Of course I did, fool!" snapped Doctor Frankenstein. Due to Ygor's increasingly halting and accented speech, the doctor, rather unfairly, had taken to calling him "imbecile," "fool," and the like. "What has happened is obvious! For some addle-headed reason of your own devising, you came down and unlocked it! Why? To torment him further?"

"No! Eez not true!"

"Silence! Then, having carelessly or deliberately let my creation escape, you locked the door after the fact and summoned me to witness his 'mysterious' escape! Pathetic! There is no value in keeping you on as my assistant."

Ygor was devastated. Whereas before he'd been eminently employable (and not unattractive to the opposite sex) he well knew that with his current physical problems, he would now be lucky to get a job mucking horse stalls.

"Doctor Fronshtein! Not make Ygor go! Please!" he pleaded, unthinkingly adopting his new nickname.

"Enough! You will pack your imbecilic belongings and be gone by sunup! If you are here when I return, I shall call Inspector Krogh and tell him your true identity. As it is, your bungling has made me dangerously close to missing my wedding."

Now, if that wedding reference seems to come out of the blue, well, we can't help it, because it's a fact. Believe it or not, Doctor Frankenstein was indeed getting married that very night. It was the "social event" Elizabeth had been planning, to take place at his father's estate. Having now cut the timing rather close, Frankenstein raced up the steps, hitched up the mule, and lit out for Dunkelhaven.

Ygor remained staring sadly into the Monster's empty cell. But eventually, ever obedient, he limped upstairs and began packing his imbecilic belongings.

CHAPTER FOURTEEN

Rolf and Hermann headed across the valley, determinedly (we would never say doggedly) following the faint scent of the Monster. It was an erratic trail which they lost and picked up time and again. Finally, near sundown, the scent became more definite. They eagerly followed it along the bank of the creek. As the creek neared town, it widened and deepened, slowed by a weir the locals had built. The weird word "weir" is what foreign people like Germans and Brits call a small dam with water running over the top.

The cat duo knew they were close to the no-longer-dead human. They slunk silently, warily, following their noses, heeding their ears. But before they actually saw him, they stopped short, for they smelled and heard something new. A young girl human was nearby.

They peeked through foliage into a clearing. Sure enough, they saw both things their other senses had identified.

A smiling little girl in a frilly sun dress was seated on the grass by the creek. Her name was Maria. The Monster was kneeling in front of her. Each was holding a small bouquet of flowers.

"You have those and I'll have these," said Maria, cheerily.

Hermann glanced at Rolf, "Doesn't she realize that the no-longer-dead human is dangerous?"

"Young girl humans tend to be rather incautious," Rolf pointed out.

"True. Even when they don't know you they're usually good for a pet and a treat."

The Monster was completely captivated by Maria. She was far and away the nicest thing that had happened to him since being sewed together, jolted by lightning, attacked by cats, jailed, and (allegedly) burned by Ygor.

"I can make a boat!" Maria giggled, and she tossed one of her flowers into the water, where it floated delicately.

The Monster imitated her, leaning forward and tossing one of his own flowers. He smiled and grunted happily at the sight of it floating beside hers.

But Rolf and Hermann were made happy by the sight of something else entirely. As the Monster leaned forward, the fob of Doctor Frankenstein's watch dangled enticingly from his jacket pocket!

"At last! This time it will work!" whispered Rolf. "Same plan as before. When he leans forward again, we will leap together, claws full out! The tick-tock will be ours!"

He glanced excitedly at Hermann, but was alarmed to see his compatriot had an un-focused, eyes-winced expression. "I'm afraid now *is* the time," said Hermann, his voice strained.

"That's what I just said!"

"I mean, it is at last time for me to rid myself of my burden. Those few bites of ham seem to have set things in motion."

"What?! You can't wait *one* minute? At this the — the time of times!"

"Afraid — not — dear — friend," grunted Hermann, and he ducked deeper into the brush behind them. Cats do not, if there is any possible way to avoid it, do their kitty business in the presence of others.

Flustered, Rolf looked back at the Monster and Maria. She'd just flung her last flower. He was about to throw *his* last flower — the last time he would lean over with the watch fob dangling!

Rolf dropped into launch position, paws evenly spaced, eyes locked on target, muscles primed, butt wiggling.

The Monster leaned forward, tossing his flower.

Rolf rocketed toward him!

Unfortunately, at the same time, Maria leaned sideways, reaching for a dilapidated flower on the ground that she'd ignored before. That put her directly between Rolf and the Monster, and Rolf slammed into her back at full speed.

He clambered onto her head in a desperate attempt to get past her. Understandably, Maria was perturbed — well let's be honest, she was totally freaked. She screamed and jumped up, grabbing at the unknown thing-that-had-attacked. Staggering wildly, she managed to catapult herself right into the creek.

As we've noted repeatedly, cats are fast. Before Maria ever hit the water, Rolf had bounded off, aiming as best he could at the Monster. But his leap was a long shot at best. He tumbled end-over-end, distressingly un-cat-like, and struck the Monster in the face with an embarrassing part of his anatomy. The Monster swatted him aside with painful force, and Rolf continued his end-over-end journey in a new direction, crash-landing in the brush, knocked senseless.

The Monster, extremely tired of these cat-assaults, stalked toward helpless Rolf, and most certainly would have ended the cat's time on earth. But the Monster was stopped by a gurgling peep from behind him. He glanced back to see little Maria struggling wildly in the water, being swept downstream — and sinking!

We can't explain what he did next. We apologize, but here's why. If Doctor Frankenstein's experiment had gone according to plan, it would have been hanged-man Dedrick's brain that was reawakened. We know quite a bit about him, but, unfortunately, we know next to nothing about the abnormal brain that had been stored at the college all those years. We have no idea what sort of life it led before being removed, pickled, stolen, re-installed and rudely zotzed with electricity.

Therefore, we cannot explain why the Monster now threw himself headlong into the creek and surged downstream in a heroic effort to save Maria. Perhaps he had been a father himself? Brother to a beloved sister? Or was he just an all-around abnormal humanitarian? We just don't know.

Regaining consciousness, Rolf staggered woozily to the creek bank and watched the swimming Monster disappear around a bend. As he sighed in futile frustration, Hermann trotted up to him, grinning, "I can't tell you how much better I feel!"

"Do you? Oh, *do* you?" bellowed Rolf. Had you been here, instead of there, one of us might have succeeded!"

"Succeeded in what?" He looked around, "And where are the no-longer-dead human and the girl human?"

"I hate you, Hermann!" snarled Rolf.

"Dear me! That's — a rather strong statement," said Hermann, genuinely hurt.

Rolf immediately felt regret, "I'm sorry, Hermann. It's just that the tick-tock has escaped us again."

"And you feel my momentary absence was contributory?"

"I do."

"Well, I sincerely hope that is not the case, and I most humbly apologize if it is."

"Thank you. And I apologize for my rash and untrue statement."

"Accepted."

"That said, the tick-tock is on its way downstream."

"Downstream? As in 'in the creek?'"

"Yes. Long story."

"No matter, we must follow it. Come! I'm feeling very light-of-foot and relieved-of-spirit at the moment."

They raced downstream. No sooner had they rounded the bend when, with a great startling splash, the Monster burst up in the middle of the creek, holding the spluttering little girl high in one huge hand. Fighting the current, he flung her toward the bank. She landed with a thump and, after sucking in a huge gasp of air, burst into tears.

Rolf and Hermann dashed past on either side of her, following the Monster as he was swept further downstream. Up ahead, the weir loomed, the water rushing over it in an oily waterfall. Before he reached it, the Monster was sucked under by devious currents. The cats stood utterly motionless, staring intently at the roiling surface.

"Do you think he's drowned?" asked Hermann, worriedly.

"I don't know!"

"What if he goes over the waterfall? What will we do?"

"I don't know!"

"If he drowns, and goes over the falls, do you think he'll float back to the surface, like normal dead things? That is, I mean, in time for us to swim out, get the tick-tock and make it to the ship? Or, given that he is already an abnormal formerly dead thing, do you think he'll —?"

"Hermann!" snapped Rolf, "Do you mean these annoying questions to be rhetorical?"

Hermann thought about it, then admitted, "I don't know!"

Hermann's concerns proved unjustified. The Monster was very much alive. He erupted from the water right in front of the duo like some gargantuan crocodile that had been lying in wait for prey. His yellow eyes were fixed on them. His scarred hands grasped and grabbed and pawed. Only their speed and the fact that his hands were wet allowed them to slip through his deadly grip.

They sped toward Dunkelhaven. The Monster vaulted from the water and charged after them.

As they ran, Hermann observed between pants, "I feel like those poor mice, running from that monstrous no-longer-dead Schmutz!"

"Pray that we run as well as they!" said Rolf.

Escape System Two was employed, though with rather more hysteria than usual, since, while the Monster fell into the category of Larger-Than-Cats, he also created the new sub-category: Large, Extremely Terrifying, and Remarkably Fast for a Mostly Human.

The first opportunity to gain a lead came just before they reached town — at Baron Frankenstein's estate. They veered toward its high stone wall and actually ran straight up it like furry insects. Being very scared helped.

The Monster glimpsed them go over the top of the wall. He was delayed, but not deterred. Nothing mattered more to him now in his new life than wreaking revenge on these feline harpies who had been attacking him from the moment he first woke. He prowled along the wall, seeking a spot where he could climb up.

Inside the well-kept grounds, Rolf and Hermann caught their breath and listened to the unsettling heavy footsteps of the Monster just beyond the wall, clearly searching.

Rolf whispered, "Keep moving. We'll, find a hiding place."

Hermann hesitated, "But, you keep saying we must get the tick-tock. Is not now our chance?"

"No, now is *not* our chance," Rolf declared. "Now he is trying to kill us. We must wait for him to calm down, when we can take him unawares. That is the cat way. No need to add to our difficulties by approaching him when he is still angry."

"Ah, I agree," agreed Hermann quickly.

And as the welcome evening gloom deepened the shadows around them, they struck out across the grounds toward the rambling, ivy-covered mansion of the Frankensteins.

CHAPTER FIFTEEN

We've not said much about Elizabeth, Doctor Frankenstein's fiancé, because, frankly, she did nothing of importance — until now. But her brief role in the events of this last fateful night literally affected the lives of everyone else involved. Her role consisted of screaming her nutty head off. This came about as follows.

Rolf and Hermann padded cautiously toward the mansion. One always had to be careful approaching a human house. One never knew when it might have a huge Mastiff, Wolfhound or Great Dane lying about.

In this case, careful listening, sniffing and spying confirmed there were no dogs. So Rolf and Hermann moved closer, at last spotting an open window on the ground floor, its curtains gently rippling in the night breeze.

"Perfect." said Rolf, "We'll go inside."

"Inside the house?" asked Hermann. "Humans don't like finding us in their houses. And the fancier the house, the angrier they get."

But Rolf, as always, had a theory, "It is the lesser of unappetizing solutions, dear Hermann. I think normal humans will dislike that no-longer-dead human as much as we do. Ergo, I predict he will be afraid to enter the house. Additionally ergo, I am certain it is safer to enter a house containing normal humans than to remain outside with that non-normal one."

"I am less certain, but I hope you are right, dear Rolf."

And they leapt cat-silent through the open window. They hoped it was a bedroom. Throughout the town, in warmer months, when windows were left open, they'd often snuck into bedrooms for a nice relaxing night's sleep, safe from dogs, owls, hawks and other annoyances. They could easily come and go without waking the sleeping humans.

Fortunately, it was a bedroom. Unfortunately, it was Elizabeth's bedroom. And, you will remember, she and Doctor Frankenstein were to be married this evening. Thus, Elizabeth was not asleep in bed, but was instead surrounded by hand maidens bustling thither and yon, preparing her for the Big Event.

Rolf and Hermann landed softly, unnoticed. But they were stunned to see so many women.

"Feathers!" exclaimed Rolf.

"Feathers and hair-balls" agreed Hermann.

They side-stepped quickly and scooted under Elizabeth's large satin-draped bed.

"What is going *on* here?" worried Hermann. "Why on earth are a mass of female humans crammed into one sleeping room?"

"I'm sure I don't know," admitted Rolf, wondering how many more times he would have to say this formerly unfamiliar phrase.

"And look what that one's wearing!" Hermann rushed on. "It stretches like — like a snake clear across the room!" He was referring to Elizabeth's wedding gown, which did indeed have a train that stretched, like he said, clear across the room. Back in those days, rich people could hire a lot of extra hand-maiden types to keep track of long trains and other things of that ilk.

"It's of no matter, no matter," Rolf assured Hermann. "The main thing is, we are safe here, hidden under this bed, until the no-longer-dead human forgets about us."

"Yes, yes. And for that I am grateful," said Hermann. Having reassured one another, they picked nice spots under the bed in which to curl up and rest.

Outside, however, their luck was not getting any better. The Monster was creeping steadily toward the house. Here, again, it's a shame we don't know the history of his brain. But we can surmise that it was capable of being analytical. Once he'd found a way over the wall, the Monster had studied the grounds of the estate. There were many places in which cats *could* hide, but somehow he knew there were few places in which cats would *like* to hide. Thus, before beginning an exhaustive and likely fruitless search of the grounds, the Monster had examined the house. He had noticed the fluttering curtain in the window of Elizabeth's room. And then he had spotted a tuft of Hermann's orange fur, rim-lit in candle-light, caught on a splinter of the window sill. Thus, the Monster had quickly deduced where Rolf and Hermann were. And that's why he was now creeping steadily toward the house.

In the bedroom, Rolf and Hermann were curled up, hoping to rest, their ears trained on the open window. But as they tried to listen for suspicious noises, they found the chatter and movement of Elizabeth's hand maidens annoying.

"I wish they'd stop all that chatter and movement," said Rolf.

"As do I, dear Rolf," said Hermann. "It makes it hard to listen for the footsteps of the no-longer-dead human. I mean, if he should be nearby, which I'm sure he is not," he added quickly, if not convincingly.

Soon, Rolf got his wish. Elizabeth suddenly shoed all of her hand maidens out of the room. Rolf was immediately pleased, but had he known where this would lead, he'd have wished he hadn't wished his wish.

What the cats didn't realize was that Elizabeth was quite agitated. You see, she was that sort of person who is forever having foreboding premonitions. The trouble with people like this is that they announce their premonitions over and over, day after day, year after year and, almost inevitably, something bad eventually *does* happen. Then they pronounce, with extreme self-righteousness, that they knew it was coming all along. Beset with a current cluster of premonitions, Elizabeth had now called Doctor Frankenstein to her room.

When the door opened, the cats were floored to see him. "It's that awful human who assembles dead humans and cats!" said Hermann. "What is *he* doing here?"

"Shh!" shushed Rolf. "I'm sure I don't know. But I do know it's best we remain undetected. Don't move!"

Elizabeth stepped quickly to Doctor Frankenstein and, in a tearful voice, explained that she was sure the worst imaginable things were about to happen (this on her wedding night, mind you). Now, given her tendencies, you could say this was Elizabeth's lucky night since, after years of disaster prediction, she was destined to be absolutely "right" about the disasters that soon unfolded.

For his part, Doctor Frankenstein understood her fears as well as any man understands anything a woman says tearfully, which is to say, not very well. In a typical male way, he patiently assured her that he wouldn't let anything bad happen. However, after promising this, he did something rather atypical — he led her, by the arm of course, over to her dressing table, then stepped out and locked her bedroom door from the outside. Presumably he was concerned for her safety, but, if so, he apparently hadn't given any thought to her room's large, open, ground floor window.

Not particularly reassured, Elizabeth began to pace nervously, dragging the long train of her wedding dress back and forth past the bed. This was intensely tantalizing to Rolf and Hermann because cats simply must chase anything that dangles or is dragged around.

"Oh! I so want to pounce on that!" whispered Rolf, as the train swished past within inches of his twitching paws.

"Don't!" pleaded Hermann, "She will surely see you!" But he, too, fought to resist the delicate white cloth sweeping to and fro.

While the cats strove to control primal instincts, the Monster was in fact looking in through the bedroom window, watching for a good opportunity to enter. He waited until Elizabeth's back was to him.

The cats heard the soft thud of his step. They spun around under the bed and saw his massive boots.

"It's *him*!" gasped Hermann.

"Impossible!" co-gasped Rolf.

Elizabeth, lacking cat hearing, had no idea anyone had joined her until her pacing happened to turn her toward the Monster.

And that brings us to the part where she started screaming.

In her defense, there were pretty good reasons to scream. First of all, no woman likes discovering a man in her bedroom uninvited. Second, the Monster was really, *really* appalling, being seven feet tall, wet, dirty, stitched, cat-scratched and so on.

Though bothered by her screaming, the Monster was of course completely uninterested in Elizabeth, for he had just glimpsed Hermann's tail under the bed. He stomped toward it.

"He sees us!" hissed Hermann, correctly. The cats backed quickly out the opposite side of the bed — and into Elizabeth's absurdly long train, becoming hopelessly tangled.

The Monster saw this and now lurched toward the train, arms outstretched hungrily. Of course, to Elizabeth, this looked like he was lurching toward *her* hungrily. So she screamed all the more, circling away from him toward the door.

Rolf squinted through the gauzy train, "She's going to the door! Be ready, dear Hermann! She'll open it and we shall fly out as fast as bats!"

"Bats?" Hermann was upside down, squirming mightily in the folds of cloth.

"You know, very fast."

But Elizabeth couldn't open the door because, you'll remember, it was locked from the outside. She yanked and pulled uselessly. And screamed.

No doubt the Monster, knowing that her screams would attract attention, wished she would just shut up and get out of his way. He kept trying to maneuver past her toward the hated cats in the train behind her.

Meanwhile, frantic Rolf and Hermann realized Elizabeth wasn't opening the door. "What is the matter with her?!" cried Hermann.

"I'm sure I don't know!" replied Rolf. "And I'm getting sick of admitting it! Any three-year-old human can open a door!" It was beyond the cats' understanding that one's husband-to-be could decide to lock one in one's own bedroom.

By now you've long since been wondering what on earth Doctor Frankenstein, Baron Frankenstein, the many house servants and the fifty or sixty wedding guests were doing all this time. Well, we don't know about most of the people, but Doctor Frankenstein and some of his friends were in the wine cellar, because one of them had said he heard a suspicious noise down there. So Elizabeth got a very good scream work-out before they finally heard her and raced back upstairs.

In the bedroom, Elizabeth had given up on the door and was backing helplessly away from the Monster. Flopping around in her train, Rolf and Hermann managed to keep her between them and him. She accidentally stepped on Hermann's tail. He yowled like a banshee, but could not compete with Elizabeth for sheer volume, so no one except Rolf heard him.

The Monster grabbed Elizabeth, intending to push her aside, but then he heard Doctor Frankenstein and his party hurriedly unlocking the door. With an angry "Raaaarh!" he gave up his cat pursuit and stomped to the window. The men burst into the room just in time to glimpse him climbing out.

Out-of-breath Elizabeth collapsed into Doctor Frankenstein's arms. Rolf and Hermann finally got free of her train and scooted out the door, unseen.

They scurried down the hall. But as they rounded the corner they came face to face with a distraught maid. She was using a long-handled brush to clean cobwebs from the massive cobweb-prone beams in the hall ceiling. She was not only distraught due to the previous screaming by Mrs. Frankenstein-to-be, but also because Baron Frankenstein had spoken crossly to her earlier, saying she wasn't being diligent enough about cobweb removal. So she was mostly distraught over the possibility of losing her job. We mention all this to explain her reaction at seeing Rolf and Hermann suddenly bounding toward her.

She screamed her nutty head off. She knew they were cats and not rats or raccoons anything. But she also knew that they didn't belong in the house; and if they were found in her presence she might get blamed for them being there. When you have a job in a high-stress work environment, that's how you learn to think.

So, screaming almost as loud as Elizabeth, she dashed at them, swinging her cobweb brush like a pike.

Rolf and Hermann skidded on the polished wood floor (freshly waxed due to more wedding prep) and did a sloppy but rapid U-turn. They successfully avoided getting clobbered and raced down the hall the way they'd come. They zipped back past Elizabeth's bedroom and around another corner. Luckily, big estate-type places have lots of halls with lots of corners, so they quickly managed to lose the maid.

As they ran, Hermann complained, "I *told* you we should never have hidden in a fancy house!"

"I still contend it was our best course in light of the relentless pursuit by the no longer dead human," said Rolf defensively.

"He found us anyway!" Hermann pointed out.

"True. However, did he not then run at the approach of normal humans? Were we not spared his attack?"

"I suppose," Hermann admitted.

"Just so," said Rolf, happy to win an argument even during a life-and-death run. They ducked through the next available open door, hoping to find a nice, much quieter hiding place.

The door happened to lead to the mansion's kitchen, where they were faced with a large, distraught cook. He wasn't in the least distraught about Elizabeth's screams, for he had barely heard them. He was distraught for a reason all his own. There were more wedding guests than the number for which he'd been told to prepare. Thus, he was afraid he might run short of food, and he was sure that Baron Frankenstein would be furious if he did. Therefore, he was in no mood to see two mangy cats in his kitchen — we have to be honest, Rolf and Hermann did look mangy, at least on that night. With a guttural war cry the cook grabbed a huge meat cleaver and attacked!

From Rolf and Hermann's perspective, this was an even more extreme overreaction than the maid's. Normally, when seeing a stray cat, humans tended to wave their hands and say "Shoo," or "No, no, that's a bad kitty."

But there was no denying that this human they'd never met was attacking with intent to kill. A variation on Escape System Two was immediately employed. They split up, zooming on either side of the cook and made for an open window behind him. Even though their moves were perfectly executed, it was close. The cook's cleaver dug deep into the window sill with a nasty SNICK sound, just missing Hermann's tail as he sailed out the window.

Landing outside, they headed for the estate's surrounding wall. As they bounded over it, they glanced back to make sure the cook was not pursuing. He was not.

When they came down on the other side, they glanced everywhere else to make sure they had not inadvertently escaped into the clutches of the Monster. He was nowhere to be seen.

They ducked under a concealing bush and panted softly. Then, Rolf offered a rare apology to his friend. "While I stand by the tactical logic of my earlier decision, I confess to you, my prognosticatorial Hermann, I did not foresee the level of outrage the humans of this particular house display."

Though Hermann did not know what "prognosticatorial" meant, he recognized a compliment when paid.

"Thank you, dear Rolf."

They sat together and licked their ruffled fur. As they did so, the dreaded church bell chimed the late hour.

They groaned in unison.

"The ship is ever-closer to sailing!" said Hermann.

"Yes," said Rolf. "And we are still faced with our original goal. We must pursue the no-longer-dead human."

"But he is still angry at us!" lamented Hermann.

"I know, I know. But hopefully, having been frightened by normal humans, he will be less angry."

"Hopefully," sighed Hermann.

And so, with a few extra licks and a few paw strokes over their ears, for it is important to keep one's ears properly combed, they set off again on the trail of the Monster.

CHAPTER SIXTEEN

There was a *lot* of other stuff going on that Rolf and Hermann didn't know about. For example, they didn't know that little Maria, whom the Monster had saved from drowning, had eventually stumbled her way home — wet, grubby and crying hysterically. Her father, of course, held her close and asked what had happened. As kids do, in her blubbering, she mixed up key details of the story. The "big ugly man" got mentioned a lot. But the furry critter that had jumped on her and actually knocked her into the water got left out entirely. When she was done, it sounded to dad like the "big ugly man" had thrown her into the creek, even though that's not what Maria meant to convey.

Scooping her up, her father immediately set off to report this outrage to Inspector Krogh. By the time he got to town, exhausted Maria had fallen asleep and was hanging, wet and limp, in his arms.

In the town square, people were wildly celebrating the upcoming marriage of Doctor Frankenstein and Elizabeth. Bands were playing and there was much singing and drinking and dancing and drinking and cooking and drinking and eating and drinking, because, a) it was an excuse to party, b) the Baron was footing the bill, and c) it's always a good idea to convince rich people you're happy about their good fortune.

Everyone was having a great time since no one yet knew that the groom had recently created a monster or that the bride had been "attacked" by it. So imagine what a downer it was when, through the middle all these singing, dancing, cooking, eating and drinking people, came Maria's dad carrying his wet, limp daughter. The people he passed assumed she was dead. That misconception eventually got cleared up, but, regardless, the very idea that some ugly, seven-foot-tall homeless guy had chucked an innocent little girl into the creek made people furious. The whole crowd immediately set off for Inspector Krogh's office to demand action.

That would have been bad enough but, you remember, Acker and Eckhard were back in town. At first meaning to go to Inspector Krogh themselves, they had found that, due to the festivities, a lot of free beer was being handed out. So they had paused, for quite some time, outside a local *bierwirtschaft* to imbibe. They were still sitting there, with Annalise curled up at their feet, when Maria's father passed by carrying his "dead" little girl. Once they'd heard his story, they realized Fate had, this time, handed them all the proof they needed.

They raced with the crowd to Inspector Krogh's office. Annalise loped along eagerly behind them. Having recovered from the shock of seeing the Monster and Schmutz, she was feeling guilty that she'd given up hunting Rolf and Hermann. Now she hoped that her humans had found some new clue on their own, something humans occasionally did.

Once at Krogh's office, Acker and Eckhard circulated, spreading the word that they knew where the ugly giant had come from — *Frankenstein's watchtower*! For good measure, they added that they knew for certain the Monster was terrorizing the whole countryside. That wasn't true at all, but it sounded like something a monster would do, and once people are angry they'll believe just about anything.

The young man from the tavern, who had earlier sipped beer derisively in response to Acker and Eckhard's accusations, now called out in a very different tone, "I say we take up torches, pitchforks, and other hastily improvised weapons, track the Monster down and deal with it most harshly!" By the way, he was the first to refer to Doctor Frankenstein's handiwork as "the Monster," but he never got credit for it, until now.

Cries of "Yah!" "Jah!" and other German equivalents of enthusiastic agreement rose from the ever-more-rankled populace. And, in hardly any time at all, these normally bucolic folk were eagerly carrying torches, pitchforks, rakes, hoes, swords, guns, and some mysterious but lethal-looking blacksmith tools.

Ironically, Doctor Frankenstein was in the same mood as the crowd. Convinced that his creation had attacked high-strung Elizabeth, and with his wedding night in shambles, he and his father also raced to Inspector Krogh's office to demand help in tracking down the, well, you know, the Monster. When they got there, they were quite surprised to find a torch-and-pitchfork posse already assembled. Baron Frankenstein mistakenly attributed this to how well-liked he was in the community.

They consulted with Inspector Krogh, but found him shaken and inde-cisive, since nothing remotely this extreme had ever happened in Dunkel-haven before. So, the doctor and the Baron took charge. They divided the townsfolk into three groups and named them "search parties" because it sounded more civilized than "lynch mobs." They each took command of one party and put Krogh in command of the third. Everyone then stormed out of town.

Acker and Eckhard, dragging Annalise with them, joined Doctor Frankenstein's group and pushed their way to the front, because they were still hoping to enforce their private agenda.

"Herr Frankenstein," Acker called. "Lead us to the watchtower! We feel sure the Monster has returned there!" Of course they didn't feel anything of the sort. They were just hoping someone, anyone, would get them into the watchtower, where they still believed the cats to be.

But Doctor Frankenstein derided their suggestion, "He's not at the watchtower you fools! He was just at my father's estate. Now he's ter-rorizing the whole countryside! Haven't you heard?" Acker and Eckhard grimaced to hear their lies quoted back to them. They had little choice but to follow along with the mob in hopes that it might eventually go to the watchtower.

Heading out of town, Frankenstein's party passed the Frankenstein es-tate. There, the Baron ordered his entire household staff to join in the hunt for the Monster. Contrary to what you might think, the cook and the maid were quite happy to do so. It was much better than being wor-ried about punishment for failure in preparing for the now-postponed wedding. They eagerly grabbed a cleaver and a torch respectively, and marched to the head of the mob.

Just past the estate, a local huntsman joined Doctor Frankenstein's group, bringing along his three well-trained hounds. They were given the Monster's scent — a strip of cloth torn from the curtains of Elizabeth's bedroom. Immediately they set up a deafening howl and dashed ahead to pick up the trail, with the wild-eyed townsfolk hot behind them.

Annalise caught up with the hounds and trotted alongside them. They were elegant dogs indeed, obviously possessed of a wealthy, caring master. She tried not to seem envious of their sleek coats, neatly trimmed tails, and lean, well-fed bodies. "What are you chasing?" she asked, hoping she sounded nonchalant.

The hounds shot her a haughty glance. She could tell that *they* could tell she was not possessed of a wealthy, caring master. The lead hound answered tersely, "A human with a most unusual odor. And you? Are you not on the same hunt?"

"Me? Er, no."

"Then why are you here?" asked the second hound.

"I'm — chasing cats."

"*Cats?*" the hounds sniggered in unison.

"It's what my masters have requested," said Annalise. "We all do what masters demand, don't we? They've set me on the trail of the cats, Rolf and Hermann."

The hounds' sniggering stopped instantly and the lead hound exclaimed, "The *Hated* Rolf and Hermann?"

Annalise was taken aback, "I, uh, well, we don't like them in my part of town, but I didn't know that animals from your part of town even knew of —"

"We *all* despise them!" growled the second hound. "Why, they once sneaked into our owner's house and ate his prized parrot!"

"And they once infiltrated our kennel and stole food from our puppies!" said the third.

The lead hound glanced at her down his long, perfectly formed nose, with his large, clear brown eyes. "Then, you are Annalise? The Huntress?"

"I — yes, I mean — the who?"

"We hear of you from every animal we meet! From animals who have never before spoken to dogs. It's incredible. We wish you success on your fabled mission, fellow hound!"

Annalise was now positively glowing. She had never felt so proud in all her life.

"And, I might add," added the lead hound, "you are rather attractive, in a rough and tumble sort of way."

They bounded elegantly onward. Annalise slowed nearly to a stop. "Rather attractive?!" With a lopsided ear and burrs in her fur? Was he serious? She smiled to herself. No matter. It had been very nice to hear. She hardly even felt it when Acker smacked her on the butt yelling, "Get moving, you lazy cur!"

CHAPTER SEVENTEEN

Rolf and Hermann were well ahead of the search parties, and on the Monster's trail. Annoyingly, it led them up into the bleak, rocky hills above the town. No animal in its right mind went up there except birds, chipmunks and those stupid red deer. Worse yet, the trail became difficult to follow. As before, they had to track and backtrack to stay with it.

The reason the Monster's trail was erratic was, probably, that he was at a loss what to do next. His short-term goal had been to punish the cats who'd tormented him. Failing that, he'd been frightened by the people bursting into Elizabeth's bedroom. Now, to the best of our knowledge, he was just wandering aimlessly. We can be pretty sure he was pretty confused, since pretty much all of his short new life had been pretty disagreeable. After all, he didn't know where he was, why he was or, possibly, even *who* he was.

No doubt he heard the howling of the hounds in the distance. And surely he knew this was a bad sign, for he climbed higher among the rocks so he could gaze down at the night-draped valley. Far below he saw the torches weaving about, flickering in the blackness like living stars — and coming ever closer to the rocks in which he hid. He growled menacingly, something he was really good at.

On a rock ledge above him, two pointy-eared shapes appeared, outlined in iridescent moonlight. Rolf and Hermann stared down at the Monster as he stared down at the search parties.

"There he is!" said Rolf, trying to sound happier about it than he really was.

"Yes, he is there!" said Hermann, mimicking his partner's fake happiness.

There were a few rugged footpaths through the rocky hills. Hiking up one of these, Doctor Frankenstein's lynch-search party was, unknowingly, closest to the Monster's hiding place. But as the men moved along the treacherous trail, one of them fell and badly twisted his ankle. Doctor Frankenstein, eager to continue the chase, assigned a few men to stay and care for their comrade, ordering the rest to follow him.

Here, we must remind you that just about everybody in the group was drunk. We point this out in order to explain why what happened next happened. Doctor Frankenstein headed bravely on up the trail — but *nobody* followed him. Everybody stayed with the injured guy, all assuming somebody else was following Doctor F.

The next thing the doctor knew, he was alone. Even so, still upset over his catastrophic wedding night, he randomly started climbing a very steep rock face and, wouldn't you know, climbed right up to where the Monster was hiding.

The Monster watched his approach, his face darkening. He recognized Doctor Frankenstein as the man who had been there when he awoke in the laboratory. That man, he knew, had something to do with his current wretched state. As Frankenstein climbed higher, the Monster sank lower.

On the ledge above the Monster, Rolf and Hermann could not see Doctor Frankenstein, and were earnestly working up their courage. Rolf whispered, "All right, *this* time is the time of times. We pounce together! Claws out, front and rear! With eight paws combined, we cannot fail to snag the chain of the tick-tock!"

Hermann eyed the Monster worriedly, "Is there not possibly some *other* plan?" he asked timidly.

Rolf wished there were, but stated the obvious, "While we are in many ways the pinnacle of creation, we are, nonetheless, cats, and therefore have few options available for this rather unique circumstance."

Hermann sighed, and for the umpteenth time summed up his courage.

"We pounce together!" he gritted, trying to keep the tremor out of his voice.

They crouched. But then Rolf hesitated, glancing at his partner.

"And no delays this time, Hermann! When I leap, you leap!"

Hermann was a bit miffed, "I told you, dear Rolf, I have rid myself of my former burden. I am fully fit and ready."

They re-crouched, and they were but a split second from leaping when Doctor Frankenstein suddenly climbed into view, searching about with his torch.

Rolf and Herman's tails drooped. "Feathers!" hissed Rolf, "Him *again?!*"

"Maybe he's looking for his tick-tock?" offered Hermann.

The doctor wandered right past the Monster's hiding place, and the Monster stepped out behind him. Frankenstein whirled. They stood staring at one another. Then the Monster lunged forward and struck Frankenstein a single, powerful blow. Frankenstein toppled instantly, knocked cold, his torch falling to the rocks with a shower of sparks.

"Oh my!" whispered Hermann.

"Well, he shouldn't have come up alone," sniffed Rolf. He's had ample evidence the no-longer-dead human is dangerous. After all, he put it together."

"True, true."

The Monster scooped up Doctor Frankenstein as though he weighed nothing and carried him off.

Hermann shook his head wearily at this, yet another unexpected turn of events, "*Now* what do we do?"

"We — we follow," said Rolf. "Again. Some more."

And they did.

Some distance away, the tipsy members of Doctor Frankenstein's search party had finally noticed they had lost their leader, and began searching for him. The hounds got a whiff of the Monster; and Annalise got a tantalizing whiff of Rolf and Hermann. With a chorus of harmonic howls, they all started off in the same direction.

The search party raced after the hounds. Acker and Eckhard raced after

Annalise, hoping that she was still looking for the cats and not just caught up in the excitement.

The Monster, and again we admit it isn't clear what he was thinking, inexplicably carried Doctor Frankenstein out of the hills and straight toward the old windmill, whose great sails were spinning ominously in the moonlight. Did he mistake the mill for the watchtower? Was he just looking for any hideout? We don't know.

Oh, and we must digress here to explain why the windmill was spinning so late at night (ominously or otherwise). There had been a bumper crop of wheat the previous year, and some had been stored through the winter for grinding in the spring. With warm weather arriving, and the price for fresh flour soaring, the mill's owner had decreed that his employees were to grind grain any time the wind blew, day or night.

Since the wind was in fact blowing, there was a disgruntled young man on duty at the mill, dutifully grinding the wheat. He was disgruntled because he had hoped to take a certain lady friend to the big party for the Frankenstein wedding. However, not to be thoroughly thwarted in his amorous designs, he had arranged to meet his sweetheart by the mill pond so they could be together for at least a little while, sip some wine and — talk.

He had just slipped out of the mill for that meeting when the Monster came along lugging Doctor Frankenstein. So he didn't see the Monster enter the mill and bar the door behind him.

Rolf and Hermann were following, slinking through the grass. The mill's gear-driven innards were clanking, creaking and groaning. Cats, being very sensitive to noise, don't like creepy sounds, but Rolf fought to keep them on task, "The moment we see our chance, we pounce!"

"Pounce! The moment!" echoed Hermann.

Just then a horrific shape rose up in front of them! Caught by surprise, given that they'd thought the only horrific shape in the area was inside the mill, they hissed and spat as loud as they could, bouncing sideways with backs arched and fur spiked to maximum.

Then they saw that the horrific shape was Schmutz. He looked at them with a sad expression, and said in a soft, hurt tone, "Why you hiss and spit at a brother cat?"

Realizing they'd made a grave mistake, Hermann spoke up instantly, again taking charge in a way that surprised both Rolf and himself, "Because — because — we were practicing! We did not know you were there. Our sincere apologies, brother cat, who is so very similar to us in practically every way."

"Ah," said Schmutz, not completely convinced.

Seeing that, Hermann quickly changed the subject, "So, brother cat! How fare you in your hunt for the mice for whom we so completely share your hatred?"

Schmutz jerked his scarred head at the windmill and grumbled, "They escape me into strange-smelling human house with arms that move and that makes frightening noises. No hole in it big enough for me to follow. So I wait. Then, no-longer-dead human came. And he bring evil human who made us. I afraid of them, so now I hide."

"Ah, and very wise, too, to hide. We suggest you continue hiding and — and I am sure your patience will be rewarded," vamped Hermann.

Schmutz made a soft "Raaarh" sound which was uncannily like the "Raaarh" sound the Monster made. But he nodded agreement, drew back behind a bush, and began licking his naked, rat-like tail.

Shaken, but relieved, Rolf and Hermann continued to the mill. Indeed, there was no opening large enough for the bulky Schmutz, but they quickly spotted a normal-cat-sized gap at the corner of a sagging window shutter. They leapt through it.

Once inside, they hid behind a sack of wheat, of which there were dozens, for this was the grain floor, where the grain was stored prior to milling.

They scanned about, but the Monster and Doctor Frankenstein weren't on this floor. Just as they spotted the stairs to the next level, they heard in the distance, even over the grating and rumbling of the mill, a bell. But it wasn't the sonorous gong of the church bell. It was different, more faint, high pitched. And suddenly they knew —

"That — that is the *ship's bell!*" cried Hermann.

"Yes," said Rolf darkly, "and it will not ring many more times before the ship sails! We must move faster than fast, dear Hermann."

They hurried up the stairs, ears locked forward, paws stepping ever so lightly; and came to the meal floor, where flour poured down through two chutes in the ceiling, falling into large bins. The air was thick with flour dust which began to coat their fur. But there was no one here, either. They would have to search higher.

They went up more steps to the next level, called the stone floor. It was even louder and more nerve-wracking than the floors below, because here two vertical drive shafts turned the two great horizontal millstones. Grain was pouring from the floor above down into holes in the stones' centers. Fresh-ground flour was gushing from their outer edges into troughs where paddles pushed it into the chutes leading to the room below.

Still seeing no one, and giving all that scary equipment a wide berth, they moved to the next set of stairs. These were so steep they were almost a ladder, leading to an open hatch in the floor above. Rolf and Hermann climbed side by side, and slowly poked their heads up through the hatch.

This was the top floor of the windmill, circular and cramped, and made even more claustrophobic by its inward sloping walls. The only light came from the sickly orange flame of a sputtering whale oil lamp perched precariously on a narrow window ledge. It had been left there by the young mill worker, so that if his boss should happen look at the mill from town, he'd see the lamp and know that his employee was conscientiously grinding grain and not having any sort of fun.

But the low light level was the least of the cats' concerns. This room was the most distressing of all. It was where power from the wind was transferred to the millstones below, so it was jammed with spinning gears and cogs and shafts and what-nots, all of them making a deafening racket. Even worse, the entire room itself periodically shuddered, groaned, and *turned.* This was due to a thing outside called a fantail, which, via more noisy gears, automatically rotated the top of the mill to face the wind whenever the wind changed direction.

The cats flattened their ears and cringed as the room dizzyingly grated through a quarter turn. Where an engineer would say, "Fascinating!" and a child might say, "Cool!" Hermann said, "This place is possibly worse than the room of lightning!" Rolf agreed.

But now, adding outright fear to the general tension, the cats spotted their quarry. The Monster was across the room, staring out another small window. Seeing the torches of the approaching search parties, he made his threatening "Raaarh" sound, fitfully waving his hands as though to banish his pursuers.

The cats ducked behind the big grain bin which fed the wheat to the millstones on the floor below. They peeked out, one head above the other. Now they also saw Doctor Frankenstein, lying unconscious on the floor.

The Monster's back was to them. Rolf drew down into pounce position, "This is really, *really* time, Hermann!"

Hermann drew down, resolute, "The time of times, Rolf!"

"Ready?"

"Ready!"

"Now!"

They sprang upon on the Monster's back, clawing and scratching like demons, swiftly working their way to his front in hopes of snagging the watch chain.

Unfortunately, this leap was still not the time of times. The Monster, rather attuned to cat attacks by now, instantly spun around like an angry top (if you can imagine a seven-foot tall human-shaped top). Rolf and Hermann were just as instantly thrown off.

Rolf artfully counter-rotated his tail and arched his back, managing to land on his feet. Hermann, less quick as always, slammed headlong into that whale-oil lantern, knocking it off the shelf, *then* spun his tail, arched his back and landed on his feet. The lantern crashed to the floor and broke. The whale oil spilled out. The sputtering wick lit the oil — and flames slowly began to spread.

Hermann dashed over and joined Rolf against the wall. The Monster stalked toward them. They were on the side opposite the entrance. There was no where to run.

"What do we do? What do we do?" whispered panicked Hermann.

"Leap again!" replied Rolf in a shaky voice. They both knew it was suicide to leap straight at the Monster's open hands. They both knew there was no other choice.

Now, while we've often noted that luck was not with our duo on this adventure, that wasn't strictly true at this precise moment. For Doctor Frankenstein chose this precise moment to come to. He flopped over right between them and the Monster, causing the Monster to pause.

He regarded them blearily and said, barely mouthing the word, "Cats?" He knew there was something he should remember about cats, but couldn't bring it to mind. And you have to give him a break, what with the failed experiment, disastrous wedding night, getting clobbered and kidnapped and so on.

As Rolf and Hermann shrank back, the doctor heard a threatening grunt behind him and turned to see the Monster looming. That took precedence over the unexpected-cat issue and he immediately thought about escape. Spotting the open floor hatch, he crawled for it. The Monster responded angrily, commenting, "Raaaaaaaarh!"

Frankenstein crawled more vigorously. But the Monster stomped over and grabbed him. They wrestled. Frankenstein resisted mightily, and as he did so, his fingers caught on the watch chain. The watch was neatly plucked from the Monster's jacket pocket, flew across the room and landed right in front of Rolf and Hermann.

The cats stared at it.

Hermann said, "That's —"

And Rolf said, " — the tick-tock!"

Rolf snatched the chain in his teeth and added, jaws firmly clenched, "I musht shay thish moment goesh a long way toward offshetting our previoush run of bad luck."

"It does, Rolf. It does."

"Let us away!"

And they awayed quickly down the hatch.

Meanwhile, Doctor Frankenstein broke free from the Monster and dodged behind clanking gears in the center of the room. The Monster was momentarily confused, not sure which direction to go in order to recapture the doctor. They looked balefully at one another through the whirling machinery.

Below, Rolf and Hermann scampered past the rumbling millstones. But as they reached the next flight of stairs, five tiny shapes suddenly sprang out in front of them. Rolf and Hermann skidded to a stop.

It was the mouse family.

"You're *alive*!" cried Hermann, genuinely pleased.

"No thanks to *you*!" snapped Mother Mouse.

"Shh!" snapped Father Mouse.

"Shh, yourself!" retorted Mother Mouse. "The thing, Schmutz is still out there! We are trapped in this nightmare place, unable to return to our beautiful monster-free home!"

Rolf's eyes narrowed into a dark glare. He had no use for the mice now. Hermann saw his claws extend.

But before Rolf could strike, a tiny voice, even tinier than that of Father and Mother Mouse, squeaked, "Is that the *angel*?"

The voice came from one of the infinitesimal, pink mouse babies, clinging to Mother Mouse's fur. He pointed upward with his little pink snout. Everyone turned to look.

He was indicating the light from the fire started by the fallen lamp, flickering weirdly through the course floorboards above them. It did look kind of angelic in a demonic sort of way.

"He said to wait for the light of the angel," added Baby Mouse.

"What?" demanded Mother Mouse angrily.

"He *did* say that," pointed out Father Mouse, staring solemnly up at the undulating glow.

"Yes! Yes I *did* say that," said Rolf, who had, of course, forgotten it. "It is the final sign! Now at last we can complete our spell and drive the thing, Schmutz from your home forever. Yes, complete our spell which — which we must cast from outside. So, wait here until we have cast it! Come, Hermann!"

He dashed around the mouse family and raced down the final flight of steps. Hermann hesitated, but then followed, guiltily avoiding their eyes.

On the grain floor, they raced among the sacks, heading for the window through which they had entered. As soon as they were beyond the mice's hearing, Hermann shot a judgmental look at Rolf, "That was hardly truthful."

Rolf skidded to a stop below the window and stared at his friend, "Hermann! In the name of all that is catlike, they are mice! *Mice!*"

"You might have at least told them to run for their lives."

"And have them parading about shouting 'Rolf and Hermann are liars' to everyone they meet? We've a long way to go to get to that ship, dear Hermann! We can chance no impediment."

"Even so, they've been so unflaggingly faithful —"

"Stop! Stop! You are truly starting to worry me. Can you not simply revel in the fact that we have at last achieved our goal? We can forever leave this thankless place with its hounds, no-longer-dead humans, irksome Bichons, *and* bizarre, un-educated mice!"

The ship's bell rang shrilly in the distance. Rolf gave Hermann an angry look and leapt out through the window. Hermann fell sullenly silent, but he followed Rolf.

Back up on the top floor of the mill, Doctor Frankenstein had spotted a small door behind him and decided to make a break for it. The door led out onto a narrow balcony used for servicing the windmill's fantail.

The Monster charged after him. The doctor attempted to climb over the railing, but the Monster caught him and yanked him back up. Frankenstein fought and kicked and struggled. The Monster pawed and wrestled and said "Raaaaaarh!"

Down below, Rolf and Hermann were racing away from the mill without missing a step. Then they missed several steps. And stopped dead, gaping.

For, charging toward them up the narrow trail was an absolute *army* of torch-and-weapon wielding humans. The three search parties, now combined, were following the hunter's hounds.

Of particular significance to the cats, however, was that the cook and the maid from Baron Frankenstein's estate were at the forefront of the furious mob. The cook spotted Doctor Frankenstein and the Monster on top of the mill. He pointed with his cleaver and cried out, "There they are!" The maid beckoned with her torch and the crowd surged forward!

Rolf and Hermann were utterly aghast, for they assumed the cook had been pointing at them. Hermann whispered in terrified awe, "Were there *that* many people in that fancy house?!"

Rolf was thoroughly abashed. He hung his head and lamented, "I say again how right you were, dear Hermann. The humans of that house harbor a fury toward cats beyond all imagining. How can they hate us so? We are so elegant, and clean, and cuddly! *So* much better than dogs, birds and turtles! Truly we are cursed in this place, dear Hermann."

"Agreed, Rolf, but now we must hide. They are completely blocking the trail and nearly upon us!"

They U-turned toward the mill. The only nearby hiding option was a rabbit hole. They dove straight down it just before the light of the torches fell upon them. There, stuffed together quite uncomfortably, they cowered as the mob stampeded overhead, footsteps shaking the earth.

Not far away, Schmutz, disquieted at the onslaught of humans and dogs, shrunk down as low as he could, huddling under his bush.

The hounds, of course, reached the mill first. As Annalise bounded along with them, she suddenly got a fresh whiff of Rolf/Hermann. Spinning about, she zeroed in on the rabbit hole and began whining and digging furiously.

The cats backed as deep as they could into the hole, but Annalise was clawing out great plumes of dirt. In seconds, she could actually see them. She howled in triumph, "I've got youuuuuuu! I've got youuuuuuu!" They were sure they were doomed.

But Acker now caught up. He kicked Annalise soundly in her much-mistreated butt. "Idiot dog! You chase rabbits at a time like this?!" Startled, Annalise yelped in pain, then whined and pointed her nose frantically at the rabbit hole. But Acker only kicked her again. Never before had Annalise wanted so much to bite a master.

Down in the hole, Rolf and Hermann shared a glance of utter surprise, "Amazing!" said Rolf. "Her idiot humans don't even realize she knows where we are!"

"I am astonished, but grateful," said Hermann.

They tentatively poked their heads up. Annalise just sullenly stalked away from the hole and sat down. It was the last straw. Till now loyal to a fault, she had officially given up. She'd made up her mind to watch the rest of the drama without getting involved in any way whatsoever.

And there was a lot to watch.

On top of the mill, the Monster and Doctor Frankenstein had continued to battle. The Monster easily got the upper hand, but then he did a rather odd thing, given that he'd gone to the trouble to carry the doctor all this way. He threw him off! Frankenstein fell only a few feet before landing, bent-over, on one of the windmill's sails. Even though that was painful, he was lucky in that it broke his fall. His weight caused the great wheel to reverse and slowly spin the other way. Thus, he rode the sail down and slid off at the bottom. As several citizens rushed to him, the Monster roared defiantly from above.

Now, let's not forget the fire started by that fallen lamp. It had grown to the point that flames were visible through the upper floor windows. The formerly level-headed young man from the *bierwirtschaft* noticed the fire, and it gave him an impulsive idea.

"Burn the mill!" he shouted. We must point out that, back in 1810, this was a pretty nutball thing to suggest. A mill took months and months to build and performed essential work for the entire countryside. But believe it or not, the whole torch-bearing crowd thought it was a great idea. They immediately began running along the base of the mill and lighting the surprisingly tinder-dry brush which happened to be piled against it. In no time at all, flames were leaping up the outside of the grand old structure.

Forgive us for jumping around but there was a lot going on at the same time. Across the valley, Ygor, most dejected, was shambling out the watchtower gate with his pathetic sack of belongings slung over his shoulder. More introspective than his disturbing new physicality might have indicated, he was contemplating why and how the powers that be had chosen to reduce him to such dire straits. He had no idea what he was going to do or where he was going to go.

What he saw next, however, at least told him where he was *not* going to go. He saw that the windmill was on fire. And, given that he'd been unfairly blamed for just about everything that had gone wrong in the last few days, he quickly made up his mind to go nowhere near the mill, lest he be blamed for the fire, as well.

So he struck out for the opposite side of the valley. And as he shuffled along, he had a thought about what might have caused the mill fire. Despite his dark mood, it brought a sardonic smile to his lips, "Theenk maybe was de cats!" he mumbled. He would never know how right he was.

At the mill, the crowd remained transfixed by the big fire. Inside, the trapped Monster could be heard making the most pitiable shrieks over the roaring flames.

Rolf and Hermann were still watching from the rabbit hole. But nobody even noticed them, except Annalise, and she just put her nose in the air and pointedly ignored them. She'd be cursed if she was going to help her idiot masters now.

"Annalise ignores us! The humans have forgotten us!" said Rolf triumphantly. "Let us away to the ship!"

He and Hermann leapt from the hole and zigzagged among the legs of the unobserving humans. But as they did so, they heard something. Yes, over all of the other chaotic noise, Rolf and Hermann heard a much softer set of pitiable shrieks.

Hermann was positively electrified, "Rolf, stop!"

Together they leapt behind a thorny bush, where Rolf impatiently demanded, "What is it?"

"Surely you hear it!"

"Hear what?" Rolf heard it, of course, but was trying to deny it.

"It's the mice!"

Indeed it was. The mice had by now realized that the "angel" was just plain old deadly fire. And they were trapped on the mill's stone floor. Flames were licking up from below and creeping down from above.

"Can't you hear their awful screams?" insisted Hermann.

"What if I can? What of it? Hermann, we are going to *miss the ship!*"

Hermann was well aware of that, but stood his ground, "The mice could have escaped had you not told them to stay."

"I simply said the first thing that popped into my head!"

"Rolf, please! You said it to keep them from escaping and telling the truth about us. And now they are trapped. And it is our fault. If we leave them to this wholly undeserved fate, how will we live with ourselves?"

"Excellent point, Hermann, but for the fact that, when Annalise's owners kill us, we won't be *alive* to live with ourselves!"

The mice screamed again, Father, Mother, and Babies — a ghostly, harmonic ensemble.

Hermann glared at Rolf in a way Rolf found most shocking and said, "The mice have been nicer to us than any other living thing in this disastrous adventure. I will not leave them!"

The distant ship's bell sounded again. They knew from past experience it would ring but once or twice more. It was nearing the last call for boarding.

Rolf and Herman's mental stand-off lasted for a full minute. But at last Rolf sighed, his breath hissing through his teeth, still clamped on the watch chain, "And I will not leave *you*, dear Hermann."

He let the watch drop to the ground. Hermann beamed, "You are the finest cat who has ever lived, dear Rolf!"

"Yes, as I have often thought," said Rolf. And together they dashed back through the mob, heading for the flaming windmill.

Along the way, they happened to run right between the legs of Eckhard, who was riveted by the sight of the blazing structure. Sensing movement beneath him, he glanced down, and was understandably astonished to see the very cats he and Acker had sought so earnestly.

Th-th-the cats!" he blurted, whacking Acker painfully on the side of the head to gain his attention.

Attention gained, Acker was also astonished. And as Eckhard lumbered after Rolf and Hermann, Acker paused to kick Annalise again, "Idiot animal! They've been right under your nose!" This time, Annalise actually tried to bite him, but Acker ran off too fast — and Annalise was immediately upset at herself for even thinking of biting a master.

At the mill, Hermann was leading the way. The window through which they had first entered was now belching flames, so he circled around the building. "This way!" he called.

Behind the mill, Hermann spotted a scraggly tree whose branches stretched toward an open window on the stone floor. He climbed up, dashed out on a branch, and made a spectacular leap through the window. Rolf followed without complaint.

They were so intent on their new mission, they did not notice that Eckhard and Acker were close behind them. And they did not know they'd just shown the thieves how to follow them into the burning mill.

Not that there wasn't some hesitation on the part of the burglars. Eckhard stumbled to a stop at the base of the tree. "They've — they've gone into the mill!"

"I see that," grumbled Acker.

"But — the mill's *ablaze*! And Frankenstein's Monster creature thing is in there, too!"

"Coward! Be cursed, all of it! We *will* have that diamond!" roared Acker. He started climbing. After a second, Eckhard nervously followed.

Inside, Rolf and Hermann were anxiously searching the stone floor for the mice. As they circled the rumbling millstones, their eyes burned and watered in the whirling smoke. The mice were nowhere to be seen.

Hermann called out, "Mice, mice! Where are you? We've come to save you!"

Suddenly, Mother and Father Mouse popped out from under one of the mill stone supports. Mother was, understandably, a bit more miffed than usual.

"The 'angel' was *fire*!" she condemned.

"Yes. It was. All part of the master plan," Hermann lied. "We're here to get you out. Where are the babies?"

Mother Mouse shoved her snout under a tin cup lying upside down on the floor and flipped it over. Hidden beneath were the baby mice, shivering with fear.

"Pick them up! Pick them up!" cried Herman. "And I will pick *you* up! Hurry, hurry!" Mother Mouse, terrified of the fire, obeyed, squeaking softly to her babies, who scurried onto her back. Then Hermann gently picked her up in his teeth, holding her by the loose skin on her neck, just as a mother cat picks up her kittens.

Father Mouse gazed up at Rolf, "We knew you would return to us!" he worshipped.

"Yes, yes, come along," said Rolf, unenthusiastically, and roughly snatched up Father Mouse.

With the crackle of flames, howling of dogs, shouting of people and cries of the Monster, Hermann and Rolf may be forgiven for not noticing something quite significant — Acker and Eckhard jumping in through the window right behind them.

In a flash, Acker grabbed Hermann! Eckhard grabbed Rolf!

"At last! At long last!" shouted Acker. He held up squirming helpless Hermann by the scruff of the neck and drew his ugly knife! However, at this highly dramatic moment —

— the ceiling caved in.

You see, seconds earlier, on the floor above, a huge beam had fallen, trapping the Monster beneath it. The weight of beam-plus-Monster shattered the floor. So, beam, Monster and floor now thundered into the room below — on top of Acker, Eckhard, Rolf, Hermann, and the mice.

Happily, no one was hurt in this catastrophe. Sadly, that was not to remain the case. Acker and Eckhard struggled up out of the debris, having lost their grip on Rolf and Hermann. The Monster struggled up out of the debris, having lost his grip on his already questionable sanity. Bruised, burned, and mistreated by everyone he'd met except little Maria, it was with considerable enmity that his yellow-eyed gaze fell upon Acker and Eckhard.

Literally at his feet, Rolf and Hermann just froze where they were, the mouse family held firmly in their mouths. Freezing turned out to be a good move. The Monster never noticed them as he lunged for Acker and Eckhard, grabbed them in his mighty hands and lifted them right off their feet, very much as they had just done to Rolf and Hermann.

Meanwhile, out in front of the mill, Schmutz was still hiding from the townsfolk. He was frightened of them, since the only humans he'd known were Doctor Frankenstein and Ygor; and this bunch, shouting angrily, waving torches and weapons, seemed even worse. So he had decided it was better to slink away and forget the mice he so longed to catch.

He was simply going to return to the watchtower, but as he began sneaking from bush to bush, avoiding the people, he happened to sneak through the very bush where Rolf had abandoned Doctor Frankenstein's watch.

Schmutz recognized it of course, and he was quite struck by the sight, for what Hermann had told him about it had lodged securely in his transplanted brain: *this pocket watch was the passport to a place where cats were treated nicely.* He thought about his solitary life in the watchtower. Then he imagined being treated nicely in some far off land reachable only by ships.

Easy decision. He promptly scooped up the watch chain in his slavering jaws — be fair, he couldn't help that they were set on permanent slaver. Then he continued sneaking along past the crowd, headed for town.

Back inside the mill, the enraged Monster shook helpless Acker and Eckhard to and fro. Rolf and Hermann remained motionless at his feet. After a few more vigorous shakes, the Monster threw the burglars right through the flaming front wall of the mill!

Outside, people ducked and screamed as the wall exploded outward in a plume of red-hot embers. Then they "oohed" and "ahhed" like people watching fireworks as the two flaming brigands flew over their heads like ungainly meteors. The pair landed far down the slope with an awful crunch, throwing up shower of red and orange sparks, quite thoroughly deceased. Later, oddly, no one remarked on this spectacular sideshow. Once people discovered the victims were only Acker and Eckhard, the consensus was that the more dramatic event was the Monster's flinging of Doctor Frankenstein, so that was the story that was later told and re-told. Acker and Eckhard were forever denied their place in this epic, until now.

But there was one observer for whom the ne'er-do-wells' end was most profound — Annalise. She was now master-less! And for a dog, losing one's master, no matter how onerous he/she might have been, is a *very* big deal. It requires serious consideration, and Annalise put her mind to it at once. The natural impulse was to return to her former owner; to show up all bedraggled, having traveled a great distance, endured untold hardship, etc. etc. But she had to be honest with herself: her previous owner was a jerk, too. So, after about one second's thought, she rejected

FRAIDY CATS

the miraculous-return scenario.

She took a guilty look around to see if anyone was paying attention, for dogs are inherently guilty about anything they do of their own volition. Then she ducked into the shadows and crept along the edge of the crowd. Rather like Ygor, she didn't know where she was going, but she knew where she was *not* going. Perhaps she would become a street dog who begs for food. She had seen other dogs do it and they seemed to get by okay. Or, perhaps she would become a hunter, just go wild! She didn't know.

Back in the mill, the Monster was glaring out through the hole in the wall he'd just made with Acker and Eckhard. The angry townsfolk were shouting and waving torches. He "Raaaaaaarhed" down at them. This was just the distraction Rolf and Hermann needed. They dashed for the window on the other side of the room. But as they reached it, Rolf skidded to a stop, pointing out —

"The tree is on fire!"

Indeed, the tree they'd climbed to reach the window was now a picturesque but highly un-navigable flame-sculpture.

"Oh, no!" cried Hermann rather uselessly, his cry muffled with Mother Mouse in his mouth.

"I would like it noted," said Rolf, his mouth also full, "that I did predict this course was suicidal."

Hermann glanced around their disturbingly enflamed environs. The Monster still had his back to them. That gave him a few seconds to think. He looked out the hole in the front wall. Just beyond it, the mill's great sails were spinning past with clockwork regularity.

With new hope he declared, "We — we will leap to the spinning arms of this strange building! We will leap just as that human did, and ride the arms to the ground!" Here he was referring to what had just happened to Doctor Frankenstein.

Rolf dryly observed, "I would like it further noted that I think the human was *thrown*. And I think he was badly hurt in the process."

"Not the point, Rolf, not the point! We have few options and we shall follow his example!" Hermann was more focused on this escape than on anything previous in his life, except perhaps eating. He watched the sails whoosh upward past the ragged hole in the wall, noting the timing.

"Now!" he commanded. And Rolf obeyed, secretly very impressed with this new Hermann. In perfect unison they dashed right past the Monster on either side, leapt through the hole, and landed bulls-eye on a passing sail, claws digging into the cloth. The sail was on its way up. However, the cats and mice were not nearly as heavy as Doctor Frankenstein, so the sail did not reverse direction and carry them down. Instead, it continued right on up, higher and higher.

"You are taking us to the sky," screamed Mother Mouse. "There is nothing in the sky except blackness and sparkles!"

"All part of the plan," stated Hermann with little conviction, his stomach churning queasily at the sight of the ground receding below. But soon the sail reached its apex and started its downward arc.

"You see!" announced Hermann. "Down we go!"

But somewhere the mill's innards, more framework was collapsing. With a deep boom, a hellish blast of flame exploded from the ground floor windows, driving the crowd back. Inevitably, each sail would now pass through the jet of fire. As they rode down toward doom, Mother Mouse screamed anew, "We'll be entirely engulfed in flames!" A bit poetic, but accurate.

Hermann and Rolf glanced around, looking for options. And cats in a tight spot can glance around faster than you can imagine. In three seconds they had both spotted a scraggly branch on a gnarled old fir tree. It was far enough from the mill to be safe from the fire. In two seconds their sail would pass near the branch. In one second they made up their minds. And jumped!

It was a grand leap, the grandest Hermann had ever made. Okay, Rolf had made grander, but we've already said he was the more athletic. The branch sagged with their weight. Twigs snapped and flew. Paws and claws scrabbled and snagged. They had made it! They raced to the very top of the old tree and sat motionless, intending to stay there till the local craziness diminished.

Down below, Annalise had just reached the rear of the crowd. But as she loped for the trail leading to town, something loped out of the brush right in front of her. It was Schmutz, setting forth with the watch.

As animals always do when facing the unknown, they froze and stared at one another, muscles tense, senses on high alert.

"What *are* you?" asked wide-eyed Annalise, having seen this hodge-podge quadruped only once before.

"What are *you?*" asked Schmutz, never having seen a bloodhound before.

Hearing the grotesque gurgle of Schmutz's voice, Annalise's fur came up, tail went rigid, and lips pulled up, showing fang.

Instinctively, Schmutz knew that those actions signaled trouble, and trouble was the last thing he wanted right now. He lowered his tail and head, tried to flatten his ear holes and said, quite humbly, "Please. No fight. I go away. Far away and not bother."

Among animals, such submissive action usually avoids a fight. And it did so now. Annalise was reassured that Schmutz was not a threat. But what he had said intrigued her: "far away."

She laid down her fur, lowered her lips and said, "Oh, well, that's all right then, but do you mind if I ask *where* you're going? Where is 'far away?'"

Schmutz, having not a devious bone in his relatively new body, simply stated the truth. "Not know. Taking this tick-tock to get on ship in harbor. Ship going to take me to a land where everyone is nice to cats."

Annalise, having no idea where to go anyway, reacted to this with more interest than she might have otherwise. "Far away" sounded better than anywhere around Dunkelhaven.

So now she dipped her head, lowered her ears, wagged her tail and asked, "Would you mind if I come along with you?"

Schmutz was actually quite nervous about his new adventure, since the only place he knew was the watchtower. The possibility of having a companion who had experience with the outside world was very attractive. Plus he didn't know what a dog was, so he didn't have that whole cat-dog bias to overcome.

He smiled, "Yes, can come with." It was a scary, toothy, drippy smile, but Annalise had seen bulldogs smile, so she knew it was sincere.

Just then there was an absolutely awful scream from inside the flaming mill. The scream came from the Monster. For he was trapped, surrounded by flame — and now, terribly, the whole huge building collapsed in a towering fireball.

Annalise and Schmutz flinched and ducked down at the tremendous noise and blast of heat. But once they saw there was no threat to them, they forgot all about it. Annalise wagged happily, "Okay! Let's go!" And off they went, side by side, headed for the harbor.

For the assembled citizens it was a little different. They stared at the destruction in awe, because there's nothing like a good burning building collapse to instill awe. They were also relieved, and even rather proud of themselves, because they'd destroyed the Monster without having to fight him directly. They had been truly scared of him, albeit for false reasons. Only later did it sink in that they were now going to have to build a whole new windmill. When they eventually did, they found that there was a pool of water under the mill, and some worried that the Monster might have survived by falling into it. We are investigating.

But at the time, everyone just went home. The huntsman leashed his hounds and dragged them away. A few men finally picked up unconscious Doctor Frankenstein. He'd been lying there all this time, of course, but everybody had wanted to stay to see the mill collapse.

High above the scene, framed against the full moon in the gnarled pine, silent and unobserved, were two cat silhouettes — with little mouse silhouettes dangling from their mouths. Rolf, Hermann and the mouse family were very happy to see the humans leaving.

"You see?" said Hermann, "We have saved you!"

Mother Mouse was more relieved than she wanted to let on, so she said guardedly, "Perhaps, perhaps. But what of the thing, Schmutz?" You had to give her credit; she was a stickler for the fine points of a deal.

But just then Rolf happened to notice movement far below them on the trail leading toward town, "Look there!"

Everyone looked. They could just make out the moon-lit shapes of Schmutz and Annalise, loping down the trail. There was no mistaking

Schmutz's distinctive lopsided gait, or the annoyingly flaunty wag of An-nalise's tail.

"As we promised!" proclaimed Rolf, "The thing, Schmutz flees from our power, never to return!" Of course, privately, he had no idea why Schmutz was leaving or whether or not he would come back, but Rolf was never one to miss milking a moment.

Mother Mouse was, for once, silent, and perhaps a little gratefully hopeful.

Hermann spoke up, "We will now return you to your home of homes, which is free of threats."

And with that, bearing their mouse burden, Rolf and Hermann scuttled quickly down the tree and trotted across the valley toward the watchtower.

Chapter Eighteen

You've no doubt forgotten all about Ygor, but we haven't, because it's our responsibility to keep track of everyone.

Following his plan, he had swung wide across the valley, as far as possible from the burning mill. This meant he would not come to a bridge over the creek until he was near town, but he didn't mind, since he didn't know where he was going anyway. He patiently followed the creek, keeping to the shadows, fearful of meeting anyone. In so doing, however, he had a mishap. He stepped in something hidden in the brush. The something was the something Hermann had left there earlier, or, one might say, deposited. And it was not as well covered as cat somethings usually are because, you will remember, Hermann had been in a rush when he deposited it. Well, anyway, the something was now smeared all over Ygor's boot.

This final injustice brought him almost to tears, "Ygor no money. Ygor no home. Ygor no job!" he rasped in his new raspy voice.

Trembling with pent up anger and sorrow, he hopped one-legged over to a log and sat down to clean the cat stuff off his boot. Fortunately, the moon was full, and he could see well enough to do the job. Even more fortunately, he could see, embedded in the stuff, an object which sparkled with startling brilliance. Ygor was a pretty educated guy and he knew full well that kitty stuff didn't have things in it that sparkle (reminder: this was long before they invented Christmas tree tinsel). So he cleaned the object off with a couple of oak leaves, then held it up to the moonlight.

It was the biggest diamond Ygor had ever seen.

"Ygor — *rich!*"

Chapter Nineteen

The pack rat was quite unnerved, for he was looking not at Rolf and Hermann, but at a bloodhound and some unspeakable *thing* from whose slavering jaws dangled the watch he so long had coveted.

"What *are* you?" he stammered, backing into the highest corner of his cluttered home, near an escape exit.

"Never mind what he is," said Annalise. On the walk to town, Schmutz had explained about Rolf and Hermann's bargain with the pack rat, and Annalise had easily found the way to the rat's home. She went on, "He has the tick-tock. You want it. So you must honor the contract and give us passage onto that ship."

Pack rats are nothing if not good business animals. After some haggling over how near Schmutz was allowed to approach, he hewed to his original agreement and granted verbal boarding passes to Schmutz and Annalise. Word was passed to the Eagle's bilge rats and, just before the ship's gangplank was raised, the two new friends scampered aboard.

CHAPTER TWENTY

Rolf and Hermann carried the mice across the watchtower courtyard to the massive front door. It was wide open. On his departure, Ygor had left it that way in a fit of passive-aggressive pique.

"We, the gods from the Outer World, now do return you to your home!" declared Hermann, as he gently set Mother Mouse and her babies on the door step.

Rolf plunked down Father Mouse beside them and mumbled, "I so thusly do likewise, *etcetera*."

Mother Mouse was silent, but Father Mouse was moved to make a speech. "This is a great day!" he squeaked. "A momentous day! A day of which all mouse-kind will sing songs of wonder and praise."

Now Mother Mouse spoke up, "We don't know any other mouse kind. They're all dead."

Father Mouse chortled slyly, "You and I are most prolific procreators. Our ever-expanding progeny will sing the songs of wonder and praise!"

Rolf refused to be impressed, "And we will wallow in the praise of the songs — but from afar. For we have many other great tasks to perform. Goodbye." He swatted Hermann on the ear, spun about and headed back into the valley. Flustered, Hermann followed Rolf, calling back cheerily to the mice, "Uh, goodbye!"

He caught up with Rolf, who stalked along, stiff-legged. Sensing that, despite their recent good fortune, his compatriot was in a foul mood,

Hermann kept silent. Not until they had reached Dunkelhaven did Rolf's more measured breathing and slight curve of tail indicate that he had calmed somewhat. Then Hermann chanced to speak.

"Really now, Rolf, all in all, don't you feel uplifted?"

"Does that feel like being insane?"

"Come, come, we've just done a marvelous thing."

"If by that you mean 'inexplicable,' I agree," said Rolf dryly. "We, who are more hungry than we have been in our entire existence, have recently carried succulent mice, *in our mouths*, back to their home and *let them go*."

"Oh, you're not going to pretend you don't grasp the significance of the circumstances."

"It is the fact that I grasp them that causes me to feel insane."

Hermann was pondering a retort when they both stopped short, noses up. An absolute tidal wave of inviting smells filled the air.

They had arrived at the town square, where the celebration of the wedding had been taking place. Huge amounts of grilled pork, venison, beef, goat, lamb, and fish were piled on plates at the various temporary food stands.

More importantly, *the square was deserted.* The town's entire population was gathered at the Baron's mansion, telling and retelling the story of the heroic hunt for Frankenstein's Monster while Elizabeth and a team of doctors tended to the injured doctor (he recovered).

Hermann and Rolf glanced all around the square, unbelieving, yet confirming that there was not a single human or guard dog to be seen. Then, eyes fully saucered, they slowly, humbly approached the greatest assemblage of food they had ever encountered.

Quite some time later, jaws aching with exertion, bellies happily aching with distension, Hermann finally re-initiated their conversation. "Now confess, dear Rolf. Do you not feel that we are somehow being rewarded for our good deed?"

"I will not deny that I enjoyed this repast."

"Excellent, and further, I must point out that said deed has, however inadvertently, led to solving our other problem. Those two unsavory humans no longer pursue us. We don't even have to leave Dunkelhaven if we don't want to."

"But I *do* want to. I've wanted to from the very beginning," said Rolf.

"That you have, Rolf, that you have," Hermann quickly acknowledged. "And in truth, I agree even more wholeheartedly than I did at the start. To think that this whole town would rise up and attack us for a minor incursion into that overblown house; when we didn't even take anything!"

"So true!" said Rolf. "It would have made more sense for them to chase that scary no-longer-dead human, or the crazy human with the tick-tock, or even the thing, Schmutz!"

"Indeed! So of course you are right. We are well to leave this place of evil and never come back."

Rolf suddenly glowered at him, "Don't think me too unmindful of our current good fortune if I point out that the ship has sailed."

"I know, I know, but another route will soon present itself."

"How are you so sure of that?"

"Because it is spring. The well-to-do humans will be pulling their carriages from the storage sheds and taking journeys to neighboring towns. We won't have to rely on the weekly coach, with its strong-armed coachman. And, now that we don't have to hide from the unresasonably vengeful Annalise or her evil now-dead humans, we can take all the time we want to canvass the horse stables and watch for the perfect carriage, one with an ideal hiding spot for two cats. We will ride in comfort to a town far, far from here — there to begin new lives!"

Immediately after his excited pronouncement, Hermann got a musing expression, "Speaking of Annalise, I wonder what happened to her — and to the unfortunately misshapen Schmutz."

"Hopefully, we will never know," sniffed Rolf.

And as far as we know, they never did. But we do, as related in the following abnormally short chapter.

CHAPTER TWENTY-ONE

We have one tantalizing hint that, many months later, Annalise and Schmutz made out quite all right. In the Eagle's log of the voyage, the captain notes that, while she was anchored in Pago-Pago, two dogs, one astonishingly ugly, suddenly sprang from the hold and raced down the gangplank, frightening crew and locals alike. The captain may be forgiven for not realizing Schmutz was a cat, but in any case, we know that the pair arrived at their intended destination. Hopefully, dogs were treated as well there as cats reportedly were. The captain also noted that, mysteriously, the Eagle's hold was completely free of bilge rats. No doubt they had met their match in the thing, Schmutz.

CHAPTER TWENTY-TWO

Returning to our primary story, Hermann's prediction about summer carriages soon came to pass. As they patrolled one of the better class stables (where they were able to steal an excellent meal from its ineffectual "guard cat") they spied a very nice carriage being readied for travel. It had a high-sided luggage rack on the roof.

Horses were hitched, a fancy-dress coachman boarded, and the carriage set forth. Rolf and Hermann eagerly followed it to one of the town's finest hotels. Very soon, fancy-dress hotel bellmen loaded the rack with several pieces of brand new luggage. Rolf and Hermann smiled at one another as they saw there would be plenty of room to hide.

The owner of the carriage came out of the hotel.

It was Ygor, for he was now a man of some wealth.

There is a curious side-note worth mentioning here. Because no one had a clue that Ygor was really Fritz, and because Ygor had appeared in town mysteriously, and because the hanged man, Dedrick, had disappeared from the gallows; a rumor began to circulate that Ygor in fact *was* Dedrick, who had somehow not died when hung. Ygor thought this was amusing and did nothing to dispel the rumor.

Anyway, as he stumped awkwardly along, he was laughing and talking with a lovely young lady. This particular lady was, as they say, of the evening, but he had persuaded her, for a fee, to accompany him on his move to the city of Ingolstadt, a much more upscale town than Dunkelhaven. As he boarded the carriage with his giggling lady friend, he did not know that the cause of both his misfortune and fortune was in the luggage rack directly above his head.

So, Ygor and the lady and Rolf and Hermann rode in fabulous comfort to Ingolstadt. The sun was just setting and a full moon just rising as the carriage passed through the city gates. The driver didn't notice the cats behind him as they poked their heads up to sniff the air of their new home.

"I smell smoked fish!" cried Hermann.

"And I smell basting chicken!" added Rolf.

They rose higher and surveyed all around.

"Look at the houses!" said delighted Hermann. "Every one is fabulous!"

"There must be hundreds of pampered pets to be preyed upon!"

"You were wise to propose we leave our previous, clearly substandard town," said Hermann, because he knew Rolf would like being reminded it was all his idea.

"Thank you, dear Hermann," beamed Rolf.

At that moment, a mournful howl arose from the woods just outside town, echoing through the streets. Frightened birds erupted from bushes. The carriage's horses reared and bucked. The coachman made the sign of the cross.

But Rolf and Hermann were unperturbed. They aimed their ears quizzically at the sound, Hermann observing, "I must say, Rolf, the local canines sound a bit *basso profundo*, don't you agree?"

"Quite so, dear Hermann. Perhaps they are all large, rotund, and slow — from being so well fed!"

The friends laughed together, thrilled with the promise of their new life in this place. For, you see, Rolf and Hermann had never heard the howl of a werewolf.

THE END